NIGHT M

The sound came again. It was the faint rasp of the window being raised.

A dark shape pushed past the curtains. He could see the intruder silhouetted against the faint light from outside. Longarm was about to grasp his revolver when something rattled and the intruder let out a yelp and pitched forward toward the bed.

Longarm whipped his hand up and grabbed the intruder's throat, finding it by blind luck in the dark. As his fingers closed around a slender neck, they both fell off the bed, landing on the rug beside it with a thump. He got his other hand on the throat and hoped the son of a bitch didn't have a knife.

It took him about ten seconds to realize . . .

Longarm let go of the woman's neck and jerked himself up off of her, exclaiming, "What the hell!"

He heard a couple of deep, rasping breaths, then she said a little hoarsely, "Is that how you always greet female visitors, Marshal Long?"

DON'T MISS THESE ALL-ACTION WESTERN SERIES FROM THE BERKLEY PUBLISHING GROUP

THE GUNSMITH by J. R. Roberts
Clint Adams was a legend among lawmen, outlaws, and ladies. They called him . . . the Gunsmith.

LONGARM by Tabor Evans
The popular long-running series about U.S. Deputy Marshal Long—his life, his loves, his fight for justice.

SLOCUM by Jake Logan
Today's longest-running action Western. John Slocum rides a deadly trail of hot blood and cold steel.

BUSHWHACKERS by B. J. Lanagan
An action-packed series by the creators of Longarm! The rousing adventures of the most brutal gang of cutthroats ever assembled—Quantrill's Raiders.

DIAMONDBACK by Guy Brewer
Dex Yancey is Diamondback, a southern gentleman turned con man when his brother cheats him out of the family fortune. Ladies love him. Gamblers hate him. But nobody pulls one over on Dex . . .

WILDGUN by Jack Hanson
Will Barlow's continuing search for his daughter, kidnapped by the Blackfeet Indians who slaughtered the rest of his family.

TABOR EVANS

LONGARM AND THE WAYWARD WIDOW

JOVE BOOKS, NEW YORK

This is a work of fiction. Names, characters, places and incidents are either the product of the author's imagination or are used fictitiously, and any resemblance to actual persons, living or dead, business establishments, events, or locales is entirely coincidental.

LONGARM AND THE WAYWARD WIDOW

A Jove Book / published by arrangement with
the author

PRINTING HISTORY
Jove edition / January 2001

For information address: The Berkley Publishing Group,
a division of Penguin Putnam Inc.,
375 Hudson Street, New York, New York 10014.

The Penguin Putnam Inc. World Wide Web site address is
http://www.penguinputnam.com

ISBN: 0-515-13001-X

A JOVE BOOK®
Jove Books are published by The Berkley Publishing Group,
a division of Penguin Putnam Inc.,
375 Hudson Street, New York, New York 10014.
JOVE and the "J" design
are trademarks belonging to Penguin Putnam Inc.

PRINTED IN THE UNITED STATES OF AMERICA

10 9 8 7 6 5 4 3 2 1

Chapter 1

This was a house of God, Longarm thought as a bullet chewed splinters from the thick wooden beam of the doorframe about six inches from his head. Fellas hadn't ought to be shooting at it.

But it was going to take more than fear of the Lord to stop the killers who were after him. Longarm brought the Winchester to his shoulder, triggered off three shots as fast as he could work the rifle's lever and pull its trigger, then ducked back into the shadows inside the old mission. He grabbed the massive wooden door and started to swing it shut as he shouted at the women, "Get back! Hunker down behind those pews!"

More slugs thudded into the door, but they weren't able to penetrate it. That door was so thick it would probably stand up to anything except maybe a cannonball, thought Longarm. He grunted as he shoved it shut with his shoulder, then dropped the bar across it that would hold it closed. Anybody who tried to come in that way would have his work cut out for him.

The mission had been built a couple of hundred years earlier, Longarm guessed, when the Spanish padres first came to this part of what was then New Spain. Not all the Indians who lived here at the time had taken kindly to being converted, sometimes against their will, so the missions had been constructed to serve as fortresses also. The conquistadors who had come with the padres had seen to it that rifle slits were cut in the walls so that they could use their matchlock muskets. Longarm was grateful for that as he ran over to one of the narrow slits and peered cautiously through it.

The rifle slit widened out on the interior of the wall so that a defender inside the mission had a better field of view—and field of fire—than folks outside. Longarm couldn't see any of the gunmen who had chased him and the women in here, but he knew they were there. He wondered if there was a back door to the mission. If there was, he and the women might be up the proverbial creek without a paddle, because he couldn't be in two places at once.

But if there wasn't, he could hold off an army from in here—at least until his ammunition ran out. The Colt in the cross-draw rig on his left hip was a .44 and used the same cartridges as the Winchester, and Longarm knew the loops on his shell belt were full. That gave him twenty rounds right there. He felt inside the pocket of his denim jacket and brought out a small box. It contained forty more cartridges, and he was damned glad he had thought to get it out of his saddlebag earlier, when he hadn't been sure exactly what he would find when he rode into this nameless little Mexican village.

So, he could hold out for a while but not forever. Not to mention the problem of food and water, which would become more important the longer they were trapped in here. Things could have been worse, but they could have been a whole hell of a lot better, too.

A rifle bullet spanged through the slit and whipped past Longarm's head. He jerked back instinctively. That had been a lucky shot, he knew, but luck could kill a man just as dead as good aim.

"Thanks, Billy," he muttered. "You sure know how to get a fella in one bad scrape after another . . ."

"You ever done any matchmaking, Custis?" Chief Marshal Billy Vail had asked a couple of weeks earlier in his office in the Denver federal building.

Longarm leaned back in the red leather chair, cocked his right ankle on his left knee, and dug a cheroot out of his vest pocket. "Can't say as I have," he replied. "Leastways, not for other people. I reckon I've made some matches of my own."

Vail grunted. His most reliable deputy's reputation with the ladies was well-known. Longarm had had more women than a dog has fleas, and as a sober, upstanding federal official and a happily married man to boot, Vail was torn between disapproving of Longarm's amorous activities and feeling intensely jealous of the rangy son of a bitch.

Longarm had known Vail for so long that he didn't have any trouble knowing what his boss was thinking as Vail frowned across the desk at him. Vail cleared his throat and picked up a folded newspaper in front of him. "Read this," he said as he tossed it over to Longarm.

"What part?" Longarm asked as he unfolded the paper. He stuck the cheroot in his mouth unlit.

"The story that starts out *Montoya Lawsuit Filed in Federal District Court.*"

Longarm scanned the dense column of type. Some of the details may have escaped him, but he got the gist of the story: Some rancher down in New Mexico named Alejandro Montoya was filing suit against another rancher named McCabe over a boundary line dispute. Such things weren't that uncommon; the only odd angle was that the suit had been filed in federal court instead of territorial court. And that was explained, Longarm noted a moment later, by the fact that this fella Montoya's holdings came from an old Spanish land grant. The Treaty of Guadalupe Hidalgo had put such things under Uncle Sam's jurisdiction.

"I don't get it, Billy," Longarm said as he lowered the newspaper. "What's this got to do with us?"

"Did you notice the date on that paper?"

As a matter of fact, Longarm hadn't. He checked it and saw that the newspaper was nearly seven months old. It had come from a town in New Mexico called Palmerton.

"I reckon I still don't see why this is any of our business."

"A couple of weeks after that lawsuit was filed, before it could come to trial, Tom McCabe was killed. Murdered, in fact. Bushwhacked while he was riding on his ranch."

Longarm shrugged. "Hard to defend yourself in court when you're dead." He tossed the newspaper back on Vail's desk and felt in his pocket for a lucifer. Finding one, he snapped it to life on his thumbnail and set fire to the cheroot before dropping the sulfur match in the bucket of sand next to the desk.

"Yep, that's why the judge postponed the case, out of respect for McCabe's widow."

"Montoya's still pressing the suit, even though McCabe's dead?"

Vail nodded. "He hasn't given up. He claims some of McCabe's range belongs to him, and he wants it back."

Longarm's eyes narrowed, and he asked, "Anybody happen to know where Montoya was about the time McCabe got himself bushwhacked?"

"He was in Palmerton, the county seat, with plenty of witnesses around."

Longarm puffed on the cheroot. "That's mighty handy for Señor Montoya, ain't it?"

"That's what some people think. The Widow McCabe and her lawyer haven't been shy about hinting that Montoya might have had something to do with McCabe's death. That's one reason things are heating up down there. Another is that the case is finally coming to trial next week."

"And you're afraid that it's liable to bust out into a shooting war before then?"

"That's what the sheriff in Palmerton thinks might happen," Vail said. "He's the one who wired me to see if I could give him any help."

"So you're sending me to keep the lid on things and let the case run its course in court?"

Vail nodded again. "That's right."

Longarm took a deep drag on the cheroot and then blew the smoke out in a perfect ring that floated toward the banjo clock on the wall. "There's just one thing I don't understand, Billy."

"What's that?"

"What in blazes does any of this have to do with matchmaking?"

"I haven't gotten to that yet," Vail said rather testily. "It seems that Montoya offered to drop the lawsuit if Mrs. McCabe would agree to one condition."

Longarm waited, but Vail didn't say anything else. Frustrated, Longarm finally said, "Well?"

Vail leaned back in his chair and laced his fingers together on his belly. "Montoya wants Mrs. McCabe to marry him," he said.

Longarm frowned. "You said her husband's only been dead for six months?"

"A little over six months. That's a respectable enough mourning period, I suppose."

"Maybe Montoya figures he won't win his case in court, so he's trying to get his hands on the McCabe range by marrying the widow."

"Could be," Vail allowed. "You can look into that, too, as well as keeping both sides from trying to shoot each other and trying to find out who ambushed Tom McCabe."

"Is that all?" Longarm asked dryly.

"Ought to keep you busy for a few days."

Longarm uncrossed his legs and came to his feet. "I'll get started."

"You can take the train to Santa Fe and rent a horse there to ride on over to Palmerton. Henry's got your travel vouchers." As Longarm turned toward the door, Vail added, "Custis."

Longarm looked back, eyebrows raised.

"Try not to shoot a bunch of folks this time," Vail said wearily.

"Now you're the one putting conditions on things, Billy." Longarm grinned around the cheroot. "I reckon I ought to be grateful, though. Leastways you didn't ask me to marry you."

Chapter 2

Longarm rode into Palmerton from the east the next day, having spent one night on the trail from Santa Fe. He wore denim jeans and jacket, a butternut shirt, and his usual black stovepipe boots and flat-crowned, snuff-brown Stetson. His big gold turnip watch, which he usually carried in his vest pocket, was in his trousers instead, along with the little .44 derringer that was welded to the other end of the watch chain. Without the vest, he didn't really need a fob for the watch, but he felt uncomfortable leaving the derringer behind. It had saved his hide too many times.

The horse he had rented in Santa Fe was a big steeldust gelding, a better mount than he'd had any right to expect to find in a livery stable. He had picked it out without hesitation when the hostler showed him what was available in the corral. Longarm had his own saddle, a McClellan, and a saddle sheath in which he carried his Winchester. He'd been able to strike a good deal with the hostler, so maybe Billy Vail wouldn't complain too much about his expenses on this job.

Palmerton was located in a broad valley between two minor ranges of mountains at the tail end of the Rockies. The slopes of the mountains were covered with pine and spruce, while the valley itself was richly grassed and had a couple of decent streams winding through it. It was fine ranching country, Longarm judged as he looked it over from the mountain pass by which he entered the valley. To the best of his recollection, he had never been here before, but he thought it was the kind of place he wouldn't mind coming back to one of these days when he retired.

Then he smiled grimly at the very thought of retirement. Gents in his line of work hardly ever got put out to pasture. They packed a badge until some badman got the best of them, and then they wound up with six feet of dirt and a stone marker.

Well, no point in dwelling on that, he told himself. If he took care of business, that sort of fate was a long time in the future. He rode down a fairly straight, well-marked trail that led to Palmerton.

The county seat was a good-sized settlement that also served as the supply point for the ranches in the valley. The broad main street was lined with businesses for several blocks. The cross streets were mostly residential, Longarm saw as he rode along slowly. The eastern end of town was obviously the respectable end. There were a couple of churches, a school house, a pair of banks facing each other across the street, a milliner's, an apothecary shop, a doctor's office, a land office, a nice-looking hotel, a restaurant, several emporiums, and a barbershop.

Smack dab in the middle of town was the courthouse, a two-story stone building. It sat not on a square as was customary, but on the south side of the street facing an empty lot on the other side. Beyond the courthouse was the less genteel part of Palmerton: a couple of livery stables, a blacksmith shop, a hotel that didn't look anywhere near as nice as the other one, and half a dozen or more saloons, ranging in size from a dingy little hole-in-the-wall to an ornate, block-long structure called the Imperial. The Imperial's batwinged entrance was on the corner, and Longarm saw several gun-hung men lounging around it. Obviously, Palmerton didn't have an ordinance against carrying weapons inside the town limits.

Longarm reined up in front of the courthouse and swung down from the saddle. As he tied the steeldust's reins to the hitch rack, he spotted a smaller side entrance with a sign over it that read SHERIFF'S OFFICE. He walked around to it, climbed up a couple of steps, and went inside. He found himself in a short hallway. To the left was a thick, heavy, padlocked door that probably led to a cell block. Longarm went through the open door on his right into a small office where almost every available bit of wall space was taken up by mounted sets of antlers.

The man behind the desk sat up straighter and grunted. "Help you?" he asked in a raspy voice. Longarm had the impression he had awakened the man.

"Sheriff Walcott?" he asked, figuring from the star on the man's vest that it was a pretty good guess.

"That's right." The sheriff pushed himself to his feet. He was a stocky man with a soup-strainer mustache and slicked-down gray hair. The black suit he wore was dusty. "Sheriff Orville Walcott. What can I do for you?"

"I'm U.S. Deputy Marshal Custis Long. Chief Marshal Vail sent me down here to see if I can give you a hand with the trouble you've got brewing."

Sheriff Walcott frowned. "No offense, mister, but you look a mite like a gunslick. You got any identification?"

Longarm reached inside his jacket and brought out the leather folder that contained his badge and identification papers. He handed over the folder, and after studying the bona fides for a moment, Walcott handed them back.

"I reckon you're who you say you are, all right. That's a relief. I thought for a second you was one of them shootists that's been driftin' into town lately."

Longarm put away his badge and papers. "You've had a run on gun-artists, have you? Any idea why?"

Walcott snorted. "I expect it's 'cause Nash Lundy sent out the word that he's hirin' gunmen."

"Who's Nash Lundy?" Longarm had never heard the name before.

"Foreman for Sam Kingston up at the Diamond K," Walcott explained. "Chief killer's more like it, I reckon. Lundy's only got calluses on one hand—the right one."

Longarm knew what the sheriff meant. A top hand generally had calluses on both hands from handling a rope and doing all the other chores that needed doing around a ranch. Most gunmen usually just worked with one hand, though.

"I don't know anything about Kingston or this fella Lundy," Longarm said honestly. "My boss told me about Alejandro Montoya and the McCabes, but that's it."

Walcott gestured at a chair covered with cracked leather in front of the desk. "Have a sit-down, and I'll tell you all about it, Marshal Long." He reached for the desk drawer. "Hooch?"

"You wouldn't happen to have a bottle of Tom Moore in there, would you?" Longarm asked as he sat down.

"Rye?" Walcott wrinkled his nose. "No offense, but I never cared for the stuff. I got some apricot brandy, though."

Longarm held up a hand. "No thanks. Maybe we'd better just go over the problems you're having down here."

"It ain't nothin' I can't handle myself," Walcott said huffily. "It's just that I figured since a federal court was involved, there ought to be a federal lawman around."

Longarm nodded. "Good thinking. Tell me about it."

Somewhat mollified, Walcott settled down behind the desk and began telling Longarm much the same story as he had read in the newspaper and heard from Billy Vail. However, Walcott was able to provide more details, such as the specifics of Tom McCabe's death.

"Tom liked to take a ride around his place every afternoon before he came in for supper. He didn't come in one evening, so his brother Warren went to look for him."

"I didn't know McCabe had a brother," Longarm put in.

"Yep. Warren's a couple of years younger than Tom was. He's not good for much, though. Sort of simple in the head. Tom always looked after him, gave him a place to live, let him work around the ranch as much as he wanted to. Tom McCabe was known far and wide as a hard man, a bad man to cross, but he always had a soft spot for Warren. And for his wife, of course."

Longarm nodded. "So Warren McCabe's the one who found his brother's body?"

"That's right. Tom was about three miles from the ranch house, at the bottom of a little draw. Looked like he'd been shot out of the saddle. Warren found the horse first, with some blood on the saddle, and backtracked it until he found Tom." Walcott shook his head regretfully. "Tom was already dead. Shot once in the back. He wouldn't have been able to tell us anything about his bushwhacker, even if he had lived until Warren found him."

"Anybody at the ranch hear a shot that afternoon?"

"Yeah, a couple. But there was nothing unusual about that. This is rattlesnake country. Hardly a day goes by that a puncher on one of the spreads doesn't have to shoot a rattler that's spooked his horse or some of the stock."

"I guess Warren McCabe brought his brother's body in?"

Walcott nodded. "Sure. He was leadin' Tom's horse already, so he tied the body over the saddle. Warren was pretty broken up about it, but he held together all right. Got Tom back to the ranch house before he sort of went to pieces."

"What happened with the lawsuit?"

"It was about to come to trial, but the judge postponed it after he heard that Tom had been killed. I heard a rumor that he called Montoya in and tried to get him to drop the suit, out of respect for Tom's widow, but Montoya wasn't havin' any of it. He wants that land he thinks is his. Judge Davis put things off as long as he could, but he'll be back around next week—he's a circuit court judge, you know, just comes through here every couple of months—and he's pretty much got to go ahead with it. He knows that Montoya's lawyer will raise holy ned if he doesn't."

"Sounds like this judge might favor the McCabe side a little," commented Longarm.

Walcott shook his head vehemently. "Judge Davis is as honest as the day is long, Marshal. He'll decide things fair and square, based on the evidence. But he's a gentleman, too, and he didn't want to put Miz McCabe through the strain of a trial unless he had to."

"Reckon it could be a mite hard on the old lady," Longarm said.

Walcott frowned but didn't say anything.

"Tell me about McCabe and Montoya," Longarm went on. "I get the feeling they'd been at odds for a long time."

"Ever since McCabe came to this part of the country, nigh on to thirty years ago. Montoya was already here, of course. His family had land grant holdings going back a hundred years or more. McCabe was one of the first white settlers in the valley. A lot of it was open land then, free for the taking to whoever could claim it and hold it. McCabe claimed some range that Montoya said was part of the old land grant. There was almost a shootin' war over it then. I was a young deputy at the time, and I remember it well." Walcott shrugged.

"Then a land commissioner came out here all the way from Washington, D.C., and studied on the matter for a while and finally said McCabe was in the right, because Montoya couldn't produce the original grant document. Montoya claimed it had gotten lost over the years, but he still insisted McCabe was squattin' on his property. It didn't do no good. Tom McCabe wasn't goin' to budge."

"Montoya didn't try to take the land back by force?"

Walcott shook his head. "Nope. Mexico was tryin' to get along with the U.S. right then, because it hadn't been long since we'd whipped 'em in the Mexican War. Montoya had relatives in the Mexican government, and they put pressure on him to abide by the Treaty of Guadalupe Hidalgo. So he backed off . . . but I don't reckon he ever forgot how his pride had been hurt. I figure that's why he finally decided to start stirrin' the pot again. He just couldn't stand feelin' like McCabe got the best of him."

"Maybe he's the one who had McCabe killed," Longarm suggested bluntly.

Walcott looked shrewdly across the desk at him. "From the way you put that, I reckon you must know that Montoya's got an alibi for the time of the killin' itself. He was here in town. I saw him myself. But I suppose he could've hired somebody to backshoot Tom McCabe. Only problem with that is, I've known Montoya as long as I knew McCabe, and neither one of 'em was the type to have somebody else do his dirty work. If Montoya wanted McCabe shot, he'd have done it himself, and from the front."

Longarm was about to point out that a hunch such as the one Walcott had just expressed wouldn't stand up as evidence in a court of law, but the sheriff was bound to know that already. Longarm decided not to waste any breath arguing. But he would keep an open mind on the question himself.

"Did McCabe's brother inherit any of the ranch, or did it all go to the widow?"

"It all went to Miz McCabe. Like I said, Warren's a good man, but not very smart. Tom probably figured his wife would do a better job of running things, and he knew she would look out for Warren just like he always did."

Longarm shifted in the cracked leather chair, which wasn't

very comfortable. "What about this fella Kingston you mentioned? Is he part of all this?"

Walcott sighed and said, "I'm afraid so. He owns the spread on the other side of McCabe's Box MCC, and *he's* got his eyes on the McCabe ranch, too."

"He doesn't have some sort of legal claim, too, does he, like that old land grant?"

"Nope, Kingston's just a greedy bastard. He showed up here a few years back, bought out a couple of smaller spreads, and started up the Diamond K. He tried to buy out the McCabe place, too, but Tom wasn't selling, of course. When Tom was killed, Kingston made noises about buying the spread from Warren, but then he found out Warren didn't inherit it. So he started pestering Miz McCabe and asking her to marry him."

Longarm sat up straighter. "What? I thought Montoya was the one who had proposed to Mrs. McCabe."

"Yep, he did, sure enough. But so did Kingston." Walcott chuckled. "And to tell you the truth, I think Miz McCabe's lawyer may be sweet on her, too."

Longarm let out a whistle. "I'll bet when her husband was killed, the old gal never dreamed that six months later she'd have three fellas fighting over her."

"Oh, you never know," said Walcott. "I reckon you'll be meetin' Miz McCabe soon enough, and then you can make up your own mind about her."

Longarm nodded. His head was beginning to spin a little from trying to keep everything straight. It was late in the afternoon now, and his stomach was reminding him that he hadn't eaten since breakfast that morning, before he broke camp. He said, "If you've got a good place to eat in this town, Sheriff, why don't we continue this over some supper?"

Walcott patted his ample stomach. "How do tamales and enchiladas and beans sound? Washed down with some good tequila?"

Longarm grinned. After the offer of apricot brandy, he hadn't been too optimistic about whatever Walcott might suggest. But he and the local lawman were clearly in agreement on this.

"Lead on, Sheriff."

Chapter 3

Sheriff Walcott turned toward the western side of town as he and Longarm left the courthouse. "There's a cantina up here a ways," Walcott said, "that has some of the best food you'll ever eat."

Longarm nodded. Their route was going to take them past the Imperial Saloon, and several of the men who had been hanging around the entrance earlier were still there. One of them caught Longarm's eye. The man was medium height, lean and swarthy, wearing a fringed buckskin jacket and a flat-crowned black hat with a band made of silver conchas. On some men, the outfit would have made the wearer look like a dandy, someone not to be taken seriously. One glance at this man's cold eyes told Longarm that wasn't the case here.

"Hello, Sheriff," the man said as Longarm and Walcott stepped up onto the boardwalk that ran beside the saloon.

Walcott nodded curtly. "Lundy."

So this was Nash Lundy, thought Longarm. Lundy carried himself like a gunman, all right. Even though he was standing with one booted foot propped casually on a small barrel, his body had a tenseness about it that said he was ready to move, and move fast, if need be. His right hand was only inches from the butt of the gun in his tied-down holster. Longarm would have been willing to bet that Lundy's hand never strayed far from that position.

Lundy looked at Longarm and smiled. "Howdy. Don't think I've seen you around Palmerton before, Stranger."

"Could be because I've never been here," Longarm replied mildly.

"It's a nice little town. You'll like it here."

"I hope so," Longarm said. He knew that Lundy wasn't really interested in this small talk. Lundy just wanted the opportunity to size him up.

Evidently Longarm didn't make that much of an impression. Lundy went back to talking to his companions, three hard-faced men who weren't as flashily dressed as he was.

Longarm and Walcott walked on past the saloon. "So that was Nash Lundy," Longarm commented in a quiet voice.

"Yep. I reckon if you've packed a badge for very long, you can see the same things about him that I can."

Longarm nodded. "He's a gunman, all right. Kingston didn't hire him to do ranch work." Longarm paused, then went on, "Lundy been with Kingston from the first?"

"Yep. He was with him when Kingston came to the valley."

"Anything suspicious about how Kingston got his hands on those spreads he started his ranch from?"

"Not a thing," said Walcott. "Those deals were on the up-and-up, I know that for a fact. Knew both of the fellas who sold out to him. One of them headed out to California, the other went back to Georgia where he'd come from." The sheriff paused, then added, "Now there *were* some questions about how Kingston built up his herd as fast as he did."

"Folks thought he might have done a little wide-looping?"

Walcott shrugged. "Tom McCabe lost some cattle; so did Alex Montoya. And so did some of the smaller ranchers in the valley. But nobody was ever able to prove anything against Kingston, and after a while the rustling stopped. Could be there was a band of desperadoes moving through the area, and they took those missing cows on somewhere else."

"I reckon you investigated at the time?"

"Damn right I did," Walcott snapped. "Never was able to come up with the cows or whoever took 'em. I'll say this, though, I never found any stock on the Diamond K with blotted brands, and Kingston was pretty reasonable about lettin' me slaughter a few beeves at random and skin 'em so's I could check."

Slowly, Longarm nodded. It sounded as if Kingston's hands were clean; either that, or he was mighty slick in his wrongdoing. Longarm figured on meeting Sam Kingston while he was here in the valley. He'd size up the rancher for himself then.

Walcott led him to a squat adobe building with a flat roof and a canvas curtain hanging in the entrance instead of a door. The place didn't look like much, but Longarm had learned over the years that you couldn't judge what sort of chuck a place served by what it looked like on the outside. As they stepped into the cantina, Longarm smelled rich tobacco mixed with the spicy aromas of something good cooking.

Several men were at a short bar on one side of the room. Long red and green chiles hung from strings tied to the ceiling behind the bar. More men were seated at the tables scattered around the room. They had bottles of tequila and pulque, mugs of beer, and plates piled generously high with food in front of them. An open doorway on the far side of the room led into the kitchen. The delicious smells were coming from in there.

The floor was hard-packed dirt, the tables and chairs rough-hewn and a little wobbly, Longarm discovered as he and Walcott sat down. A bald-headed man with a huge red handlebar mustache was behind the bar. He called, "And 'tis a good afternoon I'll be biddin' ye, Sheriff!"

"And the same to you, Emiliano," Walcott replied. "My friend and I are in need of some supper."

"Comin' right up." The man turned and bellowed through the door to the kitchen, "Estellita! Two dinners, *por favor!*"

Longarm leaned closer to the sheriff and asked quietly, "A red-headed Mexican with an Irish accent?"

"That's Emiliano Rafferty. His pa come over here from Ireland in the thirties and wound up a general in the Mexican army for a while, until whichever *El Presidente* he worked for—I never can keep them Mexican politicians straight—got himself unelected sort of sudden and violent-like. The general got himself and his family north of the border one jump ahead of a firing squad. Emiliano's been runnin' this cantina for the past twenty years or so. He's a good hombre."

A young woman emerged from the kitchen carrying an armful of plates and bowls with practiced ease. She came over to the table where Longarm and Walcott were sitting and began placing the food in front of them. Steam rose from the bowls of beans and melted cheese, as well as from the tortillas and enchiladas and tamales on the plates. Longarm wasn't sure what looked more mouth-watering: the food, or the girl who had brought it.

A second glance at the young woman made up his mind for him. She looked even more tasty.

Her hair was a dark red, almost copper, and fell in masses of waves and ringlets over smooth shoulders left bare by the low-cut blouse she wore. The blouse was gathered in the center of her chest, plunging low so that most of the valley between her large breasts was revealed. Longarm could see the dark rings of her nipples through the thin fabric of the blouse. She wasn't tall; he figured she would only come up to about his chin if he were standing up. But she had plenty of generous curves packed into her. The best thing about her, Longarm decided, were her eyes, which were dark and lively and full of laughter.

"What would you gentlemen like to drink?" she asked when she had finished setting the food on the table. Her voice contained an intriguing blend of Irish and Spanish accents.

"Tequila," Walcott said. "With a beer chaser."

Longarm nodded. "Sounds good to me."

"I'll tell Papa." She turned toward the bar.

"Rafferty's daughter?" Longarm asked the sheriff.

"That's right," said Walcott. "Estellita's her name. You best not get any ideas in your head about her, neither. She likes to lead on the cowboys around here and get 'em to pawin' the ground like a bunch of mad bulls. There's near been shootin' over her more'n once. But it don't do those poor moonstruck bastards any good. I reckon it's all just a game to Estellita."

"Pity," Longarm said as he watched the girl pick up a tray from the bar that contained a bottle of tequila, a saucer of salt, a couple of cut limes, two shot glasses, and two full mugs of beer. She brought it over to the table with a sashay of her hips that told Longarm the sheriff was probably right about her.

"Much obliged, Lita," Walcott told her.

"You and your friend enjoy your supper, Sheriff." Before she turned away, Lita Rafferty allowed her eyes to play boldly across Longarm, and judging from the smile she gave him, she liked what she saw. The motion of her hips, already sensuous, had a little something extra to it as she went back into the kitchen.

Walcott chuckled. "There she goes, at it already. She's just tryin' to bedevil you, Marshal."

"She did a pretty good job of it," admitted Longarm.

They began eating. The food was so hot and spicy that it had Longarm reaching for the tequila pretty often, and the liquor started a different sort of fire inside him. He took a healthy swig of the cool beer, which quieted things down a little. Eating like this probably wasn't too healthy for a fella's gut, Longarm reflected, but it sure was good.

"What's the mood of the town?" he asked as they ate. "Do most folks favor Montoya or Mrs. McCabe in the lawsuit?"

"Well, Palmerton sort of depends on all the ranches around here for its livelihood, so nobody's really taking sides. They don't want to openly back one or the other and then have that one lose. Not only that, but Alex Montoya comes from a long line of grandees, so most of the Mexes go along with whatever he says because a Montoya has always been the *patron* in this valley."

"Do the white settlers support Mrs. McCabe?"

"Not necessarily. Like I said in the office, Tom was a hard man. He had his share of enemies. Still and all, folks like to have proof, and without that old land grant, Montoya just ain't got it."

"So you're saying that the people in Palmerton and the rest of the valley are pretty much split on the question of who's right and who's wrong."

"Pretty much," Walcott agreed.

That might work in his favor when it came to keeping trouble from breaking out, Longarm thought. If the two sides were even, they might be a little more reluctant to start shooting.

Emiliano Rafferty came out from behind the bar and

strolled over to the table. "And is everything all right here?" he asked.

"You bet," Walcott said with an enthusiastic nod. He gestured across the table toward Longarm. "Emiliano, this is Deputy Marshal Long, from up Denver way."

" 'Tis pleased I am to be meetin' you, Marshal," Rafferty said as he shook hands with Longarm. "What brings you to Palmerton? Visitin' Sheriff Walcott here?"

"You could say that," Longarm allowed. He wasn't ready just yet to make the details of his job here public knowledge. He changed the subject by saying, "The sheriff told me you fixed a mighty good surrounding, Señor Rafferty. He was right. This grub's mighty good."

"Thanks. But my gal Estellita deserves most of the credit. She does most of the cooking. Her mama, rest her soul, taught her how."

"She did a good job of it." Longarm used a folded piece of tortilla to scrape up the last of the beans from his plate. He lifted it toward his mouth.

The sudden rattle of gunfire from the street outside made him drop the food and start up out of his chair. Walcott was moving, too. Side by side, the two lawmen headed for the cantina's entrance. Longarm's longer stride got him there first, and he had his hand on the butt of his gun as he stepped out into the street.

Chapter 4

Dusk was settling down over the valley, but the lamps had not yet been lit inside the cantina, so Longarm's eyes didn't have any trouble adjusting to the shadows in the street. He saw movement to his right and turned in that direction.

A man with a pistol in his hand dashed out from behind a parked wagon, triggered a couple of shots toward the Imperial, and threw himself down behind a water trough. Return fire came from inside the saloon. Bullets plunked into the water and thudded into the thick wood of the trough, but Longarm didn't think any of the shots went all the way through. The first gunman raised himself hurriedly, snapped off a shot, then ducked back down.

"Son of a bitch!" Sheriff Walcott said from behind Longarm. "They're at it again!"

"Who?" asked Longarm.

"That young fella behind the water trough is Chuy Valdez, one of Montoya's riders. He's probably got one of the McCabe hands pinned down in the Imperial."

"Looks like Valdez is the one who's pinned down."

"Yeah, but he won't stay there. He's too reckless."

True to Walcott's prediction, a moment later Chuy Valdez surged up from behind the trough and burst into a run that carried him toward another wagon. Shots from the Imperial followed him, kicking up dust around his feet. Valdez made it safely to the wagon and crouched behind one of its rear wheels.

Longarm turned to the sheriff. "You said they were at it again. I thought I was sent down here to keep this sort of trouble from starting. I didn't know there had already been shooting."

Walcott shrugged. "Ain't nobody been killed—yet."

From where he stood, Longarm could barely see Chuy Valdez, but he thought the young puncher was reloading. The gun inside the saloon had fallen silent, and it was likely that whoever had been shooting at Valdez was thumbing fresh cartridges into the cylinder, too.

Longarm had to take advantage of this lull in the fighting before it was over.

He drew his Colt and started striding out into the middle of the street.

"Hey, wait a minute!" Walcott exclaimed behind him. "What the hell do you think you're doin'?"

Longarm ignored the local lawman and kept walking. He lifted his voice and called, "Valdez! Whoever's in the Imperial! Hold your fire!"

He heard Walcott muttering "Dadgum it, dadgum it!," and then the thud of the sheriff's boots on the hard-packed street as Walcott hurried after him. A little out of breath, Walcott caught up to him and shouted, "Hold your fire! The next fella who pulls a trigger is in a heap of trouble!"

"Sheriff!" Chuy Valdez hissed from where he crouched behind the wagon wheel. "Get out of the way! That no-good Flynn will shoot you!"

"Jackson Flynn, is it?" Walcott said. "Chuy, I want you to holster your gun and come out from behind there." He turned toward the Imperial. "Jackson, you put your gun up, blast it, and come out here! I want you on the street now!"

Left on his own, Walcott might have let this fracas continue, thought Longarm, but once he had been goaded into action, he was handling things all right. Chuy Valdez and Jackson Flynn didn't know Longarm from Adam, but they knew Walcott was the sheriff and clearly didn't want to continue their fight as long as Walcott was standing between them.

Reluctantly, Valdez stood up and stepped out from behind

the wagon. His gun was holstered, as Walcott had ordered, but he looked like he was ready to grab it at a second's notice. Another young man stepped out onto the porch of the Imperial and let the batwings flap behind him. He was a typical cowpuncher, right down to the pugnacious expression on his face. His gun was in its holster, too.

Walcott said, "Now, I ain't goin' to be so foolish as to suggest that you boys shake hands and be friends. I know that ain't goin' to happen. But by gum, I want you to stop tryin' to shoot holes in each other in my town!"

Flynn pointed at Valdez. "He started it, Sheriff! He said Miz McCabe was nothin' but a thief!"

"That is not true," argued Valdez. "I said Señor Tom McCabe was the thief. I would never speak against *la Señora*, not when *El Patron* wishes to make her his wife."

"All right, all right," Walcott muttered. "Chuy, go get on your horse and ride on back to the Lariat. Jackson, you stay right where you are until Chuy's done gone, then I want you to head for home, too."

"This is not fair," Valdez protested. "I came to town for a drink—"

"Have it another time," Walcott said. "Go on with you, now."

Grumbling and stiff-necked, Valdez stalked along the street until he came to a hitch rack and jerked loose the reins of a cow pony tied there. He swung up into the saddle, cast a baleful look at Jackson Flynn, and then heeled the horse into a run that carried him out of town to the north.

Flynn started to move, but Walcott stopped him with an outthrust hand. "Not yet."

"But, Sheriff—"

"I don't want you goin' after Chuy and startin' it all over again once you get outside of town," Walcott said firmly.

"But you're givin' him a chance to set up an ambush and bushwhack me!"

"Chuy ain't a bushwhacker and neither are you. Now hush up."

Flynn looked fit to bust, Longarm thought, but the young cowboy stood there on the saloon porch and seethed quietly. Walcott had handled the situation well, defusing the violence without favoring either side. Finally, he waved for Flynn to go on, and the puncher did so, riding out of town on the same trail that Valdez had taken.

"You really think those two won't go at each other again once they're out of earshot?" Longarm asked.

"Probably not. They ain't backshooters."

Longarm remembered how Walcott had made a similar comment about Tom McCabe and Alejandro Montoya. "Somebody in these parts sure is," he said quietly. "You've got McCabe's grave to prove it."

Walcott frowned. "Yeah, I reckon you're right." He jerked his head toward the cantina. "Come on. Supper's on me, but I got to go pay Emiliano."

Longarm holstered his gun and started walking beside Walcott. As he passed the Imperial, he saw Nash Lundy appear at the entrance and rest his left forearm on the tops of the batwings as he looked out. Longarm felt Lundy's eyes watching him speculatively. Lundy probably hadn't expected the stranger in town to get between two wild young cowboys who were gunning for each other. He might be thinking that he had misjudged Longarm earlier.

Nothing wrong with that, Longarm mused. It was good to keep folks a mite off-kilter—especially a slick-fingered gunman like Nash Lundy.

According to Sheriff Walcott, the Valley Hotel on the east side of town was a much better place to stay than the Santa Fe House on the west side. "No bedbugs," according to Walcott. That was enough of a recommendation for Longarm. He rented a stall in one of the livery stables for the steeldust, left his saddle there as well, and carried his Winchester and saddlebags down the street to the hotel.

A friendly, gray-haired woman had him sign the register, then took his money and gave him a key. "Room eight," she told him. "Turn left at the top of the stairs. The room has a nice balcony."

"Thank you, ma'am," Longarm said with a tug on the brim of his hat. He draped the saddlebags over his left shoulder, carried the Winchester in that hand, and went up the stairs. He had signed in as Custis Long, from Denver, but hadn't put down anything in the register about being a lawman.

Walcott had said they would ride north up the valley tomorrow and pay a visit to both the Box MCC and the Lariat. Montoya's spread had gotten that name, Walcott had explained, because of the brand he used. It was the usual Mexican skillet-of-snakes brand, but it looked sort of like a coiled-up lariat, too, according to the sheriff.

Longarm was looking forward to meeting Montoya and the widow McCabe. Once they realized that a federal lawman was on hand, they might be more reasonable and let the judge hash things out as he was supposed to. As for figuring who, if anybody, Mrs. McCabe ought to marry, Longarm intended to steer well clear of that matter, no matter what Billy Vail had said about matchmaking. Uncle Sam didn't pay him enough for him to get mixed up in a mess like that.

The room was clean, with a nice rug on the floor and even a small vase of flowers on the table along with a pitcher of water and a basin. Yellow curtains hung over the single window. Longarm parted them and glanced out. The balcony the lady downstairs had mentioned was there, all right. Longarm frowned slightly. A balcony meant that anybody who wanted to do him harm could climb onto it and possibly get into the room that way. Of course, he didn't have any reason to think that anybody in Palmerton wanted to do him harm. Still, old habits were hard to break.

He locked the door and propped a straight-back chair under the knob. From his saddlebags he took a box of .44 cartridges and scattered them on the floor underneath the window. If anybody tried to sneak in that way in the dark, they might start slipping and sliding as the shells rolled under their feet. At the very least, the setup would probably cause a racket.

Satisfied that he had taken the necessary precautions, Longarm undressed and got into bed. As wonderful as the supper at the cantina had been, it had also been a little heavy, and he was drowsy. The tequila probably had something to do with that, too. He dropped off to sleep with his customary ease.

An unknown amount of time later, a slight noise roused him. His eyes opened, but other than that, he didn't move. His right hand was only about four inches from the butt of the gun in the holster he had hung from the bed's headboard.

He could have the Colt in his hand in less than the blink of an eye, if need be.

Unsure what had awakened him, he waited. A couple of seconds later, the sound came again. It was the faint rasp of the window being raised. Longarm had left the pane up a few inches to let in some fresh air, but now someone was on the balcony trying to open it enough to get inside the room.

Who the hell? he asked himself. He hadn't had time to make any enemies in Palmerton, and probably not very many people knew he was a lawman. Walcott had introduced him as Marshal Long to Emiliano Rafferty, though, Longarm recalled, so the fact of his identity could have spread at least a little.

Earlier, Longarm had felt a mite foolish taking precautions, but now he didn't feel that way at all. The window went up some more, and the curtains moved. They weren't just billowing from the breeze, either.

A dark shape pushed past the curtains. Longarm had blown out the lamp in the room when he went to bed, so the place was pretty dark. As the curtains parted, he could see the intruder silhouetted against the faint light from outside, but he couldn't tell anything about whoever it was. Longarm was about to grasp his revolver and call out for the person to freeze, when something suddenly rattled and the intruder let out a yelp and pitched forward toward the bed.

Longarm rolled, trying to get out of the way. He knew the intruder had slipped and fallen on the loose cartridges. Longarm wasn't quite quick enough. The intruder sprawled onto the bed, landing heavily on top of Longarm and knocking him away from the gun. Longarm whipped his hand up and grabbed the intruder's throat instead, finding it by blind luck in the dark. As his fingers closed around a slender neck, he heaved and rolled, and they both fell off the bed, landing on the rug beside it with a thump. This time, though, Longarm was on top. He got his other hand on the intruder's throat and hoped the son of a bitch didn't have a knife.

It took him about ten seconds to realize that he was lying on what felt like—and were—large, pillowy breasts.

Chapter 5

Longarm let go of the woman's neck and jerked himself up off of her, exclaiming, "What the hell!"

He heard a couple of deep, rasping breaths as the woman dragged air back into her lungs, and then she said a little hoarsely, "Is that how you always greet female visitors, Marshal Long?"

He recognized the distinctive voice, and as he picked up his trousers from the room's single chair and fumbled in the pockets for a match, he said, "Most gals don't fall on me so sudden-like, Señorita Rafferty."

"I'm sorry. I slipped and fell on something."

Those .44 cartridges, Longarm thought. They had worked just like he hoped they would, even though the circumstances weren't exactly what he had expected.

He found a lucifer and lit it. The harsh glare of the match showed Lita Rafferty sitting up on the floor next to the bed, gingerly massaging her throat where Longarm had choked her. Longarm held the match to the wick of the lamp and then lowered the glass chimney when the flame caught. A warm yellow glow filled the room.

Lita held out a hand toward him. "The least you can do is help me up."

Longarm shook out the lucifer and dropped it in the basin on the dresser. He took Lita's hand and pulled her to her feet. Despite her short stature, she was a pretty substantial gal, he discovered. She straightened her blouse, pulling it down a little so that even more of the creamy swells of her breasts were revealed, then sat down primly on the edge of the bed.

"If you don't mind me asking," said Longarm, "what are you doing here?"

"Isn't it obvious? I wanted to see you again." Boldly, her eyes took him in, ranging down from the thick mat of dark brown hair on his brawny chest to the bulge of his groin in the bottom half of a pair of long underwear, the only thing he was wearing. "And I am quite impressed with what I see."

"Compliments are always welcome," Longarm said dryly, "but climbing in a fella's window in the middle of the night is a good way to get yourself shot."

Lita shrugged, which made her breasts do interesting things under the thin fabric of the low-cut blouse. "I did not want the old biddy downstairs to know I came up here, and I thought the risk would be worth it. You would not want to prove me wrong, would you, Marshal?"

"Considering I'm standing here in my underwear, you might ought to call me Custis."

"Very well, Custis. You have the advantage of me, since you have on fewer clothes." She grasped the bottom of her blouse and lifted it, peeling the garment up and over her head. She shook the thick mass of coppery curls as they came free of the blouse. "Now, do you like what *you* see?"

Longarm liked it a lot. Her bare breasts were as impressive as he had thought they would be. Large and firm and tipped with dark brown nipples the size of silver dollars, they stood out proudly from her chest. Lita cupped them and lifted them, holding them out even farther. Then, as Longarm watched enthralled, she pushed the right breast up, bent her head, and licked her own nipple.

Longarm's shaft gave a jump and rapidly started to grow hard.

"It would feel even better if you did it," Lita said, and the huskiness in her voice this time wasn't caused by the way Longarm had grabbed her earlier.

He stepped toward her. Sheriff Walcott had warned him that Estellita Rafferty was a tease, but she didn't seem to be teasing now. She stood up as Longarm reached her. She was still holding her breasts, so he put his hands under hers and hefted the heavy globes of woman-flesh. He leaned over and snaked his tongue around the right nipple, which was already damp from her licking it. Lita sighed in pleasure.

Longarm sucked the erect nipple into his mouth and teased it with his tongue for a moment before gently closing his teeth on it. "Yes," Lita breathed as he pulled on the hard bud of flesh.

Longarm moved to the other nipple and sucked and licked it, too. Lita was breathing hard, and she let go of her breasts so that her hands could play over his bare torso, rubbing and squeezing his muscular flesh. She reached the waistband of his underwear and tugged it down. He was hard as could be now, and the underwear caught for a moment on his stiff shaft. Lita worked it free and pushed the underwear down around his thighs. She put both hands around the long, thick, blood-engorged pole and took a sharply indrawn breath. "So big," she murmured. "I must taste it."

Longarm straightened from her breasts as she sank to her knees in front of him. His erection thrust out proudly. Lita slid her palms up and down it, barely able to contain its throbbing length. She leaned forward and rubbed her satiny cheek against the head. A large drop of fluid had seeped from the slit, and it glistened on her skin as she rubbed it on her face.

She squeezed with both hands, milking out more moisture. Her tongue darted from her mouth to lap it up. Then she parted her lips wide and leaned forward even more to take the head of his shaft into her mouth.

Longarm's pulse thundered in his head. He tangled his fingers in her coppery hair and held her head steady as he began to move in and out of her mouth. She couldn't even come close to swallowing all of him, of course, but he was careful about not thrusting too much. Her tongue swirled around his manhood, and one hand reached down between his legs to cup the heavy sacs that hung below it.

Longarm knew he couldn't stand much of this exquisite torment, so after a few moments he started to pull back. Lita's hands tightened on him, and she whispered, "No! I want it this way."

A little breathless, Longarm said, "I didn't want you feeling like . . . you got the short end . . . of the stick."

"We have all night," said Lita. "I will take all you have to give me, and I know I will not be disappointed. Now I want you in my mouth."

Always oblige a lady, that was Longarm's policy. He closed his eyes and gave himself over to the sensations as she started sucking him again. His legs were trembling a little from the strain of standing there as his climax roared toward him like an avalanche.

His hips jerked, and Lita closed her lips tightly around the head of his shaft as it began to spurt. His seed boiled out of him and into her mouth. The muscles of her throat worked as she swallowed in an effort to drink in all he had.

Longarm emptied himself into her, and then she squeezed her hands along the shaft, milking out the last drops of fluid. She gave his softening organ a final, lingering lick, then came up off her knees and almost frantically pushed her skirt down over her hips and thighs. As she fell back on the bed, she spread her legs wide and said, "Now me!"

Considering the pleasure she had already given him, Longarm didn't mind in the least. He knelt beside the bed and lowered his head between her thighs. The triangle of dark red hair was surprisingly fine-spun and sparse, so that he had a good view of her sex. He used his thumbs to spread the pink folds of feminine flesh. The stiff little bud at the top of her slit demanded his attention first, so he put his tongue on it and began to move it in a circular motion.

Lita's hips bounced up off the bed, and only the fact that she jammed the ball of her hand into her mouth and bit down on it kept her from screaming so loud that she would have awakened the entire hotel. Her thighs clamped against the side of Longarm's head and pressed hard against his ears. Her back arched and she pumped her femininity against his face for a long moment as shudders of release rolled through her. Then, with a sigh, she fell back against the bed and her thighs dropped away from Longarm's head. He had seldom seen a woman come so hard, or so fast.

But he wasn't through with her yet. Not by a long shot.

His tongue darted out and slid into her, and Lita gasped in astonishment, "Oh!" At the same time, Longarm moved his right hand underneath her and speared a finger into the crack between her buttocks. Her climax had spread enough moisture down there so that his finger was able to slip inside her quite easily.

This double penetration immediately plunged her into another orgasm so strong that this time when her legs slammed against his head, Longarm thought she was going to yank it right off his shoulders. He hung on, running his tongue up and down her slit with blinding speed while at the same time his finger delved deeply into her. She arched so high off the bed that only her feet and her head and shoulders were touching the sheet.

When she finally slumped back onto the mattress, she was totally limp, and those magnificent breasts were rising and falling rapidly as she tried to catch her breath. Longarm, his senses swimming from her musk, moved up over her. He was hard as a rock again. He plunged his shaft between her drenched folds and slid it all the way inside her. Lita began tossing her head back and forth and moaning. Her eyes were closed in ecstasy as Longarm filled her.

His previous climax meant that he could last longer this time. He pounded in and out of Lita for long moments, gradually scooting her across the bed with the strength and urgency of his thrusts. He trapped her thrashing head between his hands and kissed her. Her mouth opened hungrily, so he gave her his tongue and she sucked on it desperately.

When she finally broke the kiss, she gasped, "I want to be on top!" Longarm cooperated by burying himself in her as deeply as possible, grasping her hips tightly, and rolling both of them over. Lita cried out softly as she settled down with her legs straddling his hips. She put her hands on his chest and pushed herself up so that she was sitting on him.

With her breasts right in front of him, Longarm couldn't keep his hands off them. He cupped and kneaded the fleshy globes and strummed the hard nipples with his thumbs. Lita threw her head back and thrust hard with her hips. Her small size and his more than generous endowment insured that the head of his shaft was hitting bottom inside her. She breathed in little pants and gasps of passion.

Finally neither of them could take it anymore. Longarm dropped his hands from her breasts and grasped her hips instead, holding her firmly as he drove himself up into her.

He began to spurt again, and even though it really hadn't been that long since he'd come before, his climax seemed to go on forever. He filled her to overflowing with his seed.

She fell forward, collapsing onto his chest, and for a second he was afraid he had killed her. Then he felt her heart pounding against him and felt her hot breath on his skin. He splayed his hands on her back and rubbed, massaging her and gradually working his way down to her hips. He cupped her buttocks and squeezed them as well, then affectionately trailed a finger between them. She went "Mmmm," as his organ, still buried inside her, gave a final little twitch.

She lifted her head so that their faces were only a couple of inches apart. Staring into his eyes with her dark, mischievous ones, she slowly licked her lips. "That was wonderful," she said. She started kissing his face all over, and Longarm returned the favor. They lay there, toying with each other playfully.

After a few minutes, Lita looked at him solemnly and asked, "How long will it be before we can do it again?"

Chapter 6

"What's the matter, Marshal? Didn't sleep well last night?" Sheriff Walcott asked as Longarm yawned a giant, jaw-cracking yawn.

"I was a mite, uh, restless," replied Longarm.

"I'm surprised. Miz Cochran at the hotel usually makes sure that all her guests are comfortable."

"Oh, the room was fine," Longarm said quickly. He didn't want to explain that he was sleepy this morning because he had spent most of the night romping in every conceivable position with Estellita Rafferty, so he went on, "I reckon I was just thinking about all this trouble you've got facing you."

Walcott grunted. "It could turn into a bad shootin' war mighty easy, all right. That set-to betwixt Chuy Valdez and Jackson Flynn yesterday was the worst fracas so far. But I intend to have a talk with Miz McCabe and Montoya both, and I'll read 'em from the book about lettin' their hands come into town and start slingin' lead."

The two lawmen were riding up the valley from Palmerton, bound first for the Box MCC, then Montoya's Lariat spread. It was a beautiful day, and under other circumstances Longarm would have enjoyed the ride. He appreciated good ranching land as much as anybody who had ever done any cowboying, and that had been his profession for several years when he'd come west after the Late Unpleasantness. The breeze was warm and carried a faint evergreen scent from the slopes of the mountains, the grazing was lush and green, and the cattle they passed looked fat and sassy. Puffy white clouds floated overhead in the deep blue sky. A fella could really be content here, Longarm thought.

That was when the distant crackle of gunfire came to his ears.

"Damn it!" Walcott burst out. "Now what?"

"Reckon we'd better find out," Longarm said. He heeled the steeldust into a run. Walcott rode beside him, keeping up easily on a big roan.

The trail followed the twists and turns of one of the creeks that meandered through the valley, and having to stick with that winding path slowed down the lawmen. Longarm was tempted to cut across country toward the sound of the shots, but Walcott stayed on the trail and Longarm didn't want to risk getting turned around in unfamiliar territory. The gunfire was sporadic. Longarm heard the sharp crack of at least one rifle and the flatter sound of pistol shots. A good-sized battle was going on, he thought.

The trail curved to the left in a long, fairly sharp turn. The creek bubbled and chuckled along over its rocky streambed to the right. Up ahead along its bank, a grove of cottonwoods grew. To the left, across the trail from the trees, a rocky outcropping jutted up from the ground. Longarm saw tendrils of gunsmoke drifting both from the top of the bluff and the trees opposite it.

Walcott reined in and cursed. "Five'll get you ten there's a bunch of McCabe riders up on the bluff and some of Montoya's men in the trees. We can't get in the middle of this ruckus, either, like we did yesterday evenin' in town. Too many bullets flyin' around."

Longarm agreed. He didn't mind playing long odds now and then, but he wasn't going to be out-and-out foolhardy. "We'd better split up," he suggested. "One of us can try to get behind each bunch."

"That'll expose us to fire from the other side," Walcott pointed out.

"Yeah, but we can't just sit here and let those boys keep blazing away at each other. Somebody'll get hurt for sure, if they aren't already."

Walcott nodded. "Yeah. I'll take the bluff."

"I'll take the creek," Longarm said. He veered the steeldust to the right as Walcott trotted off to the other side of the trail.

Longarm put the horse into the water. The steeldust hesitated slightly. Longarm knew that even though it was summer, the creek was fed by the runoff of melting snow from the mountains on both sides of the valley. The water was cold. The horse plunged in anyway, and Longarm rode through the shallows toward the cottonwoods.

As he came closer, he saw four horses being held on the bank by one man. That meant three men were in the trees firing toward the bluff. As Longarm splashed along the creek, the man holding the reins of the horses turned toward him. The man's hand dipped toward the revolver holstered at his hip.

Longarm used his left hand to haul on the steeldust's reins and turn the horse while his right hand flashed across his body to the butt of his Colt. He had the gun out of the cross-draw rig in a flicker of movement too fast for the eye to follow. He lined his sights on the man with the horses and called out loudly, "Hold on there, old son! Don't do it!"

The man froze with his fingers only inches from his gun. Slowly, he lifted his hand away from the gleaming ivory grips of the weapon. He wore charro pants, a short jacket, and a felt sombrero. Longarm recognized him immediately from the previous evening.

"Didn't learn your lesson, did you, Chuy?"

"Who are you?" spat out Chuy Valdez. He was literally trembling with the desire to try for his gun. Longarm hoped he wouldn't have to shoot the youngster.

It was time to really start spreading the word, he decided. "I'm United States Deputy Marshal Custis Long," he told Valdez. "And in the name of Uncle Sam, I'm ordering you to take that gun out of its holster mighty slow and careful-like and chunk it in the creek."

"No!" Valdez burst out. "I will not!"

"I reckon I'll have to shoot you, then," Longarm said.

Valdez's eyes widened. He believed that Longarm meant what he said. Reluctantly, he used two fingers of the opposite hand to lift his gun from its holster and toss it in the creek. The pistol would take some cleaning and drying before it would be usable again.

"Now haze those horses out of here," ordered Longarm.

"What?"

"Just do it!" Longarm snapped as he spurred the steeldust up out of the creek and past Valdez. He rode into the trees, hoping that no stray bullets from the bluff across the trail would come his way.

Valdez's three companions were bunched up, which made Longarm's task easier. They heard the hoofbeats of the lawman's horse and started to turn, but he was among them before they knew what was happening. He pulled his left foot from the stirrup and kicked one man in the head, sending him tumbling to the ground. At the same time he lashed out with the Colt in his right hand. The barrel thudded against another man's head, the blow cushioned enough by the man's sombrero so that Longarm didn't have to worry about fracturing his skull. That left just one man, and Longarm had him covered before the hombre could even start to lift the rifle in his hands.

"Drop it!" Longarm said as he backed the steeldust a couple of steps so that he could see all three of the men. Valdez was behind him, but the youngster was unarmed now and Longarm didn't consider him much of a threat.

He realized how wrong he was when Valdez said sharply, "No, you drop it, Marshal!"

Longarm glanced over his shoulder and saw Valdez pointing a pocket pistol toward him. Longarm bit back a curse. He had a hide-out gun of his own, the derringer attached to his watch chain, so there was no reason to think that Valdez wouldn't have one, too. Only Longarm hadn't considered that, and now he was in a fix because he had underestimated the young puncher.

He could still salvage the situation, though. Without turning around he said, "I don't reckon you want to shoot a lawman—or anybody else—in the back, Chuy."

"I will if I have to," Valdez vowed. "This is none of your business."

"I reckon it is. And I reckon you know as well as I do

that shooting me with that little pistol won't put me down quick enough to keep me from turning around and drilling you, too. It's up to you, Chuy. You can be a dead back-shooter—or you can put that gun down and listen to reason."

"Shoot him, Chuy!" yelled the man still holding a rifle. "I'll help you kill the gringo son of a bitch!" The rifle started to come up.

"No!" Valdez shouted before anybody could pull a trigger. He dropped the pocket pistol and stepped back away from it. "Don't do it, Lupe!"

The rifleman didn't listen. He jerked the rifle to his shoulder.

Longarm didn't have a choice. He squeezed the Colt's trigger and felt it buck against his palm as smoke and flame geysered from its muzzle. The bullet struck the man called Lupe high on the right arm and knocked him halfway around. The rifle spun out of his hands, unfired.

Longarm backed and turned the horse some more. "Get over there with your amigos," he told Valdez.

The two men he had knocked down were now stumbling back onto their feet. Chuy Valdez joined them and knelt beside the man Longarm had wounded. He took the bandanna from around his throat and bound it tightly around the bullethole in the man's arm. Looking up at Longarm, Valdez said angrily, "We must take him to a doctor."

"In a minute," said Longarm. He listened. No more shots seemed to be coming from the bluff on the other side of the trail. He hoped that meant Walcott had succeeded in getting the drop on those men. He asked Valdez, "What happened here? What started the shooting?"

"The same as always," spat Valdez. "Those gringo bastards from the McCabe ranch tried to kill us!"

Longarm made a guess. "The creek is the boundary between the two spreads, right?"

"*Si*. And we were on our side of the creek when they started shooting at us!"

"You're on this side now," Longarm pointed out.

"This is the closest place we could take shelter."

There was some truth to that, Longarm saw. The pasture on the other side of the creek was bare of trees for several hundred yards. If Valdez and the other vaqueros had been bushwhacked while riding over there, he couldn't blame them for lighting out across the creek and into the cottonwoods.

"How do you know it was Box MCC men who were shooting at you?"

"Who else could it be? This is their range." Valdez's face twisted in a grimace. "Even though they stole it from *El Patron*."

From the direction of the bluff, someone called out, "Hello, the trees!"

Longarm recognized Walcott's voice. He shouted back, "Everything all right over there?"

"Come on out," Walcott replied. "We'll meet you at the trail!"

Longarm gestured with his gun and said to Valdez and the others, "You heard the man."

The four Montoya men trudged out of the cottonwood grove and onto the trail, the wounded man being supported between Valdez and one of the other vaqueros. Sheriff Walcott herded three men down from the bluff. Longarm looked them over and decided he had never seen any of them before, but they were typical American cowhands. They all looked mad as hell, too, because they had been disarmed and were walking with their hands held up in the air.

"You got no right to do this, Sheriff," one of them complained. "We told you, those damned greasers ambushed us! All we did was take cover and fight back."

"That is a lie!" Valdez shot back. "It was you gringos who shot at us first!"

"Hold your horses, both of you," said Walcott. "We'll get to the bottom of this, don't you worry. I see you had to ventilate one of yours, Marshal."

"Seemed like the thing to do at the time," Longarm said. "I reckon a sawbones had better have a look at him."

"We're closer to the Box MCC now than we are to town. What say we take all those boys on up there and then try to sort things out?"

"No!" Valdez cried. "We will not go to that place!"

"You ain't got a lot of choice in the matter, old son,"

Longarm told him. "Sheriff, you want to watch these prisoners while I go round up their horses?"

Walcott nodded. "Sounds all right to me. Just don't take too long. It's gettin' on toward lunchtime, and Miz McCabe sets a nice table."

Chapter 7

Both sides in the shooting scrape stuck stubbornly to their story as they rode toward the headquarters of the Box MCC. Each claimed that they had been fired upon first. Longarm found himself wondering if that might indeed be true.

A trail branched off from the main path, crossed the creek at a low-water ford, and headed off to the east. Longarm nodded toward it as they rode by and asked Walcott, "Is that the way to the Montoya hacienda?"

The sheriff nodded. "That's right. It's about eight miles over yonder. We're goin' on to the McCabe place, though. Ought to be there in just a little while."

Walcott was right. Less than a half hour later, they rounded another bend in the trail and found themselves riding toward a large group of buildings. The most impressive structure was the huge, two-story log house that was surrounded by barns, corrals, a long bunk house, a cook shack, a smoke house, and a blacksmith shop.

"Mighty nice, ain't it?" asked Walcott. "Tom McCabe built the house with his own hands, with some help from his brother, when they first came here. It was smaller then, just a Texas-style cabin with a dogtrot between the two sides, but McCabe kept addin' on. He left the dogtrot, though."

Now that they were closer, Longarm could see that the sheriff was right. In the center of the ranch house, on the bottom floor, was a tunnellike opening, the original dogtrot.

A room had been built above it. The opening ran all the way through from front to back. Longarm had never seen another house exactly like this one.

He nudged his horse ahead so that he was riding beside the Box MCC punchers. "I reckon there's probably somebody around the place who can patch up those bulletholes in Lupe's arm?"

The men grumbled curses, but one of them said grudgingly, "Yeah, Monty Sikes—he's the boss wrangler—can treat bullet wounds just about as good as a regular sawbones. That's what he started out to be, even went to school for it, before he started cowboyin'."

Longarm nodded. "Good."

The group had been seen riding toward the ranch, and a reception committee was waiting for them. Three men had emerged from the bunk house. Two were carrying rifles, and the third had a shotgun cradled in his arms. That man strode out in front of the other two and looked up at the visitors. "Sheriff, what the hell's goin' on here?" he demanded.

"More trouble, Ed," Walcott replied. He inclined his head toward Longarm. "This here is Marshal Long, from Denver. He's a federal lawman. Marshal, this is Ed Jordan, Miz McCabe's foreman."

Longarm nodded. "Wish we were meeting under better circumstances, Jordan. Sheriff Walcott and I happened on this bunch of your men shooting it out with some fellas from Lariat."

"I see 'em," Jordan grunted. He was a stocky, middle-aged man with a graying mustache. "One of 'em's wounded, ain't he?"

"Yep. I hear tell you've got a good man here on the Box MCC when it comes to doctoring."

Jordan had the scattergun's barrels pointed toward the ground now. He turned his head and said to one of the other men, "Bob, take this fella over to the barn and have Monty take a look at his arm." Jordan glanced at Longarm. "That all right with you, Marshal?"

"That'll be fine," Longarm said. "Much obliged."

Jordan gestured at the three Box MCC punchers. "What about my men?"

Longarm looked at Walcott, who nodded. "They can go

on about their business," Longarm said. "I don't reckon they'll try to start a corpse-and-cartridge session right here in front of the main house."

"They'd damned well better not," Jordan grated. He waited a second, then said to the cowboys, "Well, what're you waitin' for? The marshal said you're free to go."

The three men didn't look overly grateful as they rode off toward the barn. In fact, they still looked as mad as wet cats, Longarm thought.

So did Chuy Valdez. "This is not fair!" he said hotly. "You let them go, yet my compadres and I are still prisoners!"

"Why don't you consider yourselves guests?" Longarm said.

"On the ranch of a thieving gringo—"

"Hush up that talk," Walcott said sharply. He nodded toward the main house. "Show a little respect, damn it."

Longarm looked at the ranch house and saw that two people had come out of it to stand on the wide porch that ran all around the structure. One was an attractive young woman with dark hair; next to her stood a tall man in a town suit, a white shirt, and a string tie.

Walcott went on, "Ed, keep an eye on these two vaqueros, will you?"

"Sure, Sheriff." The barrel of Jordan's greener rose a little.

"Come on, Marshal," Walcott said to Longarm. The two lawmen rode over to the house and brought their horses to a stop in front of the porch. Walcott tugged on the brim of his hat, nodded politely, and said, "Mornin', Miz McCabe."

Longarm realized with a shock that the sheriff was talking to the young woman. She couldn't have been more than twenty-four or twenty-five, if that old, and she had an exotic appeal about her, accentuated by the beauty mark near her wide, sensuous mouth. Her hair was black and straight and fell halfway down her back. It was parted in the middle so that it perfectly framed her olive-skinned features. She smiled, and her voice was as lovely as the rest of her as she said, "Good morning, Sheriff. I'm afraid I'm a little confused about what's going on here."

She wasn't the only one, thought Longarm. He had figured that Tom McCabe's widow would be an older woman. He had even referred to her as an old lady a couple of times when he was talking to the sheriff. No wonder Walcott had given him a funny look the first time and then seemed a little amused on the second occasion. Walcott had known that Longarm would meet Mrs. McCabe soon enough and see for himself just how wrong he had been about her.

"Well, there was a mite of trouble," Walcott told her. "Some of your boys and some of Montoya's vaqueros were blazin' away at each other, down the creek a ways. Marshal Long and I came up on them and made 'em stop shootin'."

"Were any of my men wounded?"

"No, ma'am."

Mrs. McCabe's smile widened. "Then I ought to thank you and . . . Marshal Long, was it?"

Longarm touched the brim of his hat. "Yes, ma'am," he said to her. "United States Deputy Marshal Custis Long, from Denver."

"I'm pleased to meet you, and I appreciate you helping Sheriff Walcott keep a bad situation from getting worse. I'm Emily McCabe." She put a hand on the arm of the man standing beside her. "And this is Ross Thayer, my attorney."

"Howdy," Longarm said. Thayer was a tall, sandy-haired gent with the look of a townie about him. Longarm wasn't surprised he was a lawyer.

"Pleased to meet you, Marshal. I suppose you're down here to see that justice is done in the dispute between Mrs. McCabe and Señor Montoya?"

"I'm here to keep you folks in the valley from killing each other. It'll be up to the judge to decide what justice is."

"Of course," Thayer said smoothly. "Welcome to the Box MCC."

The attorney said that almost as if *he* owned the place, not Mrs. McCabe, Longarm thought. But he supposed Thayer probably had been representing Tom McCabe before the cattle baron's murder and quite likely had been Mrs. McCabe's lawyer since then. He would be accustomed to being around the ranch.

"Did I see that one of Señor Montoya's men was hurt?" Emily McCabe asked.

"Yes'm," Walcott replied. "Your wrangler's patchin' him up now."

Emily nodded. "Monty will do a good job." She smiled

again. "Well, why don't you two gentlemen come inside? Lunch will be ready soon."

Walcott practically licked his lips. "Much obliged, ma'am," he said as he swung down from the roan.

Longarm dismounted as well and tied the steeldust's reins to one of the porch posts. He went up the steps with Walcott, and Emily McCabe ushered them inside.

The house might have been made of logs, but it was no simple cabin inside. It was luxuriously furnished, with thick woven rugs on the floor, heavy sofas and chairs, and a huge fireplace with a massive stone mantel. The walls were covered with gun racks, bookshelves, and several impressive sets of antlers. The sight of the antlers reminded Longarm of the ones in Walcott's office. The mountains on both sides of the valley must be good hunting grounds, he thought.

Longarm and Walcott gave their hats to a Mexican serving woman who wanted them. Emily McCabe said, "Please, have a seat. Can I offer you something to drink? A glass of wine, perhaps?"

"No, thanks," Walcott said as he lowered himself into one of the chairs. Longarm sat on a long sofa. Walcott went on. "We ought to talk about this trouble betwixt you and Alex Montoya."

Emily made a face. "I don't like to discuss unpleasant matters just before a meal, Sheriff. Can't it wait?"

"Well . . . I reckon it can."

"There's nothing to discuss, anyway," Ross Thayer put in. "Emily is completely in the right in this matter, and I'm confident that the judge will rule that way if he's ever allowed to hear the facts."

"You're talking about it," Emily said.

Thayer grinned and held up his hands in surrender. "Sorry."

Longarm was trying not to stare in fascination at Emily McCabe. She was stunningly beautiful, but his interest ran deeper than that. If Tom McCabe had settled in this valley nearly thirty years earlier, that would have been well before Emily was born. He had been decades older than her, and he must have married her when she was little more than a child. Why would a young, beautiful girl marry a man who was so much older than her?

No sooner had the question formed in Longarm's mind than he knew the answer: money, of course. McCabe had owned a large, successful ranch—a ranch that was now the property of his widow. Being so much younger than him, Emily must have figured that she would outlive him.

But she couldn't have figured on McCabe being ambushed and killed, and she might not have anticipated the trouble with Montoya, either. She might still wind up with everything she wanted, but it wasn't going to be as easy as she might have hoped it would be.

The only trouble with that theory, Longarm told himself, was that Emily didn't look like the sort who would have married just for money. Maybe he was giving her too much credit, but she just didn't strike him as being that mercenary.

Before he could ponder the matter any more, another man came into the room. The newcomer was considerably older, lean and tanned with a craggy face and a rumpled thatch of white hair. His face might have been severe under other circumstances, but right now he was grinning happily.

"Emily, that mare foaled this morning—" he began, then stopped short as he caught sight of Longarm and Walcott. "Oh. I didn't know we had company. Hello, Sheriff."

"Howdy, Warren," the sheriff said.

Emily came over to the man and took his arm. "Warren, this is Marshal Long," she said as she led him over to the sofa where Longarm was sitting. Longarm stood up and extended his hand. He knew this man was Warren McCabe, Tom McCabe's brother.

Warren pumped Longarm's hand and continued smiling. "I'm very pleased to meet you, Marshal," he said.

"Likewise," said Longarm. He recalled Sheriff Walcott saying that Warren McCabe was sort of simple in the head. Despite that—or maybe because of it—he was evidently quite pleasant and friendly.

Warren let go of Longarm's hand and turned back to his sister-in-law. "You really ought to come out to the barn and see the new colt, Emily. It's really pretty."

"All right, Warren," she told him. "But after lunch, all right?"

"Sure. Whenever you want to. You ought to see it trying to get around on those spindly legs—"

Before Warren could continue the story, the front door suddenly swung open. Ed Jordan, the Box MCC foreman, hurried into the room. He was still carrying the shotgun, and from the way he was gripping it now, so hard that his knuckles were white, Longarm realized something was wrong.

"Sorry to bust in like this, Miz McCabe," said Jordan, "but I figured I'd better tell you. Montoya and a bunch of his men have come callin'—and they're armed for bear."

Chapter 8

"Damn it!" Walcott exclaimed as he came up out of the chair. "Pardon my French, Miz McCabe."

"That's quite all right, Sheriff," Emily said tightly. "I understand completely."

Longarm was on his feet, too. When Emily said, "I had better go greet my other guests," and started toward the door, he moved smoothly and quickly so that he was in front of her.

"The sheriff and I will see to this, ma'am," he said. "It'll be better if you and Mr. Thayer stay inside." If bullets started flying, he was confident that none of them would penetrate the thick log walls of the ranch house.

Some of Emily's hair had fallen forward. She threw it back with a toss of her head and said, "Is this your ranch now, Marshal Long?"

"Huh? No, of course not—"

"Then I'd appreciate it if you'd get out of my way." Her eyes flashed fire for a second, then calmed somewhat. "Not that I mean to be rude."

Longarm stepped back. Maybe it would be better if Emily went to see what Montoya wanted. But he intended to stay close to her, just in case of trouble.

He had a pretty good idea why Montoya was here, too.

Hoofbeats, a lot of them, sounded as Emily marched out the front door and was immediately flanked on the porch by

Longarm and Sheriff Walcott. Ed, Jordan, Ross Thayer, and Warren McCabe trailed along behind. Longarm glanced over his shoulder and saw that the lawyer looked worried and even a little scared, but Warren was still smiling eagerly, as if he couldn't wait to see what was going to happen next.

A score of men on horseback swept up to the house. They were met by a line of Box MCC ranch hands on the ground, all of them armed and visibly tense, including Jackson Flynn, who had been swapping lead with Chuy Valdez in Palmerton the previous evening.

The riders reined in. Longarm scanned their faces and saw that every one was Mexican. One man, who rode near the center of the group, walked his horse forward. He was the oldest of the bunch, Longarm judged, and his clothing, while not fancy, was better than that of an average vaquero. His lean face was the color of old saddle leather, and his sweeping mustache was white. Longarm had a strong feeling that he was looking at Alejandro Montoya.

That guess was confirmed a second later by a cry from the barn of "Don Alejandro!" Chuy Valdez hurried forward.

Montoya paid no attention to the young man. His eyes were fixed on the group standing on the porch. He reached up and swept his sombrero off, holding it in front of him as he bowed slightly in his saddle. "Señora McCabe," he said.

"Welcome to my home, Don Alejandro," Emily said. "What can I do for you?"

"You can make me a happy man and accept my proposal of matrimony," Montoya said.

"As I've told you before, I have no interest in remarrying at the moment. I am still in mourning for my late husband."

Montoya clapped his sombrero back on his head. "In that case, I demand the return of my men that you are holding prisoner."

"Now wait just a minute, Alex," Sheriff Walcott said. "Miz McCabe ain't holdin' nobody prisoner. Marshal Long and I brought some of your men over here with us, but they ain't under arrest."

"That is not true!" protested Chuy Valdez. "They brought us here at gunpoint!"

"Just so's your compadre could get that bullethole in his arm tended to."

Valdez pointed indignantly at Longarm. "A wound that the other gringo lawman inflicted!"

Montoya stiffened in the saddle and looked at Longarm. "You shot one of my men?"

"He figured on putting a bullet in my hide," Longarm said flatly. "I beat him to it."

"You are the United States marshal of whom I have heard?"

"That's right. Name's Custis Long. Who told you about me?"

"Emiliano Rafferty's father was my friend many years ago. Now Emiliano is my friend."

Walcott asked, "How'd you know your boys were here?"

"One of my riders saw the encounter earlier this morning and watched from a distance as you forced my men to accompany you. He rode quickly to the hacienda and told me. I knew when he said you did not turn back toward Palmerton that you must be coming here."

Longarm said, "This hombre saw what happened, did he?"

"That is right, Marshal."

"And did he tell you who fired the first shots?"

A hint of a sneer appeared on Montoya's face. "The gringos, of course. They fired from ambush."

"My men wouldn't ambush anybody," Emily said. "They know I wouldn't stand for it."

"Forgive me, Señora, but you are only a woman. That is why you need a husband, to help you control your lackeys."

Ed Jordan snorted. "I ain't no damn lackey, you—"

Emily stopped him by saying, "That's enough, Ed." Her chin lifted defiantly as she looked at Montoya. "My men do what I tell them, and I've given them orders not to start any trouble. They know that they can defend themselves if someone attacks them, though. I suspect that's what happened here."

Montoya's face darkened with anger. "You dare accuse *my* men of acting without honor?" Clearly, he took that as a personal affront.

"You ride up to *my* house and accuse *my* men of being bushwhackers!" Emily shot back at him. She was just as angry now as he was. Longarm looked from one to the other of them and had the crazy thought that maybe they *should* get married. From what he could see, they were two of a kind. Emily went on, "I think you should take your men and leave."

"Gladly." Montoya looked at Longarm and Walcott and in a voice dripping with scorn and contempt asked, "Do I have your leave to go?"

"Take your vaqueros and ride out," Walcott said. "Nobody's stopping you."

Lupe and the other two vaqueros had come out of the barn by now. The wound on Lupe's arm had been cleaned and had a white bandage wrapped tightly around it. Montoya motioned curtly for his men to mount up.

Valdez and the others did so and joined the rest of Montoya's vaqueros in front of the ranch house. As soon as Montoya was satisfied that his lost chicks were back in the roost, he looked directly at Longarm and said, "I see now how much faith I can place in the American government to decide things fairly. You have already allied yourself with my enemies."

"One thing's got nothing to do with the other," Longarm told him coolly. "You'll get a fair shake from the judge, and I'll deal with anybody who tries to take the law into his own hands—on either side."

"We shall see." Montoya wheeled his horse and rode out, leading the large group of vaqueros who rode behind him.

Sheriff Walcott took off his hat and pulled a handkerchief from his pocket with his other hand. He mopped his forehead and said, "That was a near thing."

Longarm knew the sheriff was right. All it would have taken to set off a firestorm of lead was one hasty, impulsive finger on a trigger on either side. It wouldn't have mattered who started the shooting. There would have been plenty of death to go around.

"How dare that terrible old man come here and accuse me of . . . of kidnapping!" Emily said. She was still furious.

Ross Thayer took her arm. "It wasn't your fault, Emily. If the sheriff and Marshal Long hadn't brought Montoya's men here, this wouldn't have happened."

"Hold on there," snapped Walcott. "Are you sayin' me and the marshal are to blame, Thayer?"

The lawyer waved a hand. "I assure you, I meant no offense, Sheriff. It was just an unfortunate circumstance."

"Yeah, well, you get a lot of those when ever'body in the territory's so blamed trigger-happy."

Emily turned to her foreman. "Tell the men to get back to work, Ed—and thank them for standing up to Montoya with me."

Jordan ducked his head. "No thanks needed, ma'am. We all ride for the brand, and happy to do it."

Emily looked at Longarm and Walcott and said, "Well, gentlemen, I believe we were going to have some lunch." She glanced toward the fading dust cloud that marked the leavetaking of Montoya and his men. "I hope this unpleasantness hasn't ruined your appetite."

"No, ma'am," Walcott said without hesitation. "It'd take a heap more than that."

Walcott's praise of the fare at the McCabe ranch proved to be well-founded. The Mexican serving woman, whom Longarm figured was also the cook, brought out thick slabs of fried steak that were surprisingly tender, mashed potatoes, gravy, biscuits with honey, greens, and peach cobbler for dessert. It was simple food of the sort that was common throughout cattle country, but delicious nonetheless. Longarm ate with gusto, though he could see that he would never be Walcott's equal as a trencherman.

When Walcott finally pushed his chair back from the table, he sighed heavily. "That was a meal that would've done Rosaria proud, Miz McCabe. She taught you well."

"Thank you, Sheriff," Emily said with a smile. "But don't you think you should call me by my first name? After all, you've known me since I was born."

"That's true, I reckon. All right, Emily."

Longarm was seated across the table from her. He said, "Do I understand the sheriff right, ma'am? You cooked this?"

"That's right. After my mother passed away, I was pretty much raised by the woman who was the cook here on the ranch for many years. I grew up on the Box MCC."

So this ranch had always been her home, and now she was the mistress of it. That was an interesting bit of information, thought Longarm.

"What about your father?" he asked, hoping that he wasn't being too inquisitive.

"He was one of the hands. He died when I was quite young, like my mother. The men regarded me as something of the ranch mascot when I was behaving myself. The rest of the time they probably thought I was an obnoxious little brat."

Longarm couldn't imagine this gracious, beautiful young woman ever being a brat. He said, "Your parents both passed away when you were little?"

"That's right," Emily said. "My mother died of a fever when I was two. Once she was gone, I'm told that my father seemed to lose interest in living. He was killed in an accident a few months later, kicked by a horse. But I believe it happened because he was so distracted and depressed after Mother's death. I don't know for certain, of course, because I don't remember either one of them."

Longarm shook his head. "Sorry. I shouldn't have brought up such bad memories."

"They're not all bad," Emily assured him. "I've always enjoyed living on the ranch and helping Rosaria. She taught me everything she knew about cooking. And Tom was very good to me, even when I was a child. He assured me that I wouldn't have to leave the ranch, that I would always have a home here."

Walcott put in, "Some folks in the valley called Tom McCabe a shameful old goat when they heard he was goin' to marry you, Emily. Him bein' so much older than you and all."

"It wasn't like that at all," Emily said. "I was really the one who suggested to him that we get married. He thought it would look bad, too, but we loved each other. We didn't want to be apart."

Beside her, Warren McCabe began to cry.

Emily reached over quickly and took his hand in both of hers. "It's all right, Warren. I know you miss him. I do, too." She looked around the table at the others. "You see, I'm well aware that Tom had a reputation for being hard and ruthless. But there was another side to him, a side that only Warren and I saw very often. He was a good man."

"Yes, ma'am, I expect he was," Longarm said into the

silence that fell. "Otherwise a lady like you wouldn't have married him."

Walcott got to his feet. "I brought Marshal Long out here today so he could meet you, ma'am, what with the trial comin' up. We sure appreciate your hospitality, but I reckon we'd better be goin'."

Longarm wasn't in any hurry to leave, but he didn't want to contradict the sheriff. He stood up, too, and said, "Much obliged for the fine meal, Mrs. McCabe. I'm sure I'll be seeing you in town."

"Of course. Ross, would you see the gentlemen out?"

"Certainly," Thayer said. He went with Longarm and Walcott as they got their hats and walked out onto the porch of the ranch house. Pausing there, the lawyer asked, "The court date is still set for next Tuesday, right, Sheriff?"

Walcott nodded. "That's right. Judge Davis is due to get to Palmerton on Monday, and he'll convene court first thing Tuesday morning."

"We'll be there," Thayer said. "And I hope the trial won't take long. The judge should see quickly that Montoya doesn't have a legal leg to stand on."

"I hope you're right about the quick part. I'd just as soon have this all settled so folks can stop shootin' at one another."

Longarm thought the sheriff was placing a little too much trust in the judicial system putting a stop to the trouble. From what he had seen of Don Alejandro Montoya today, the old man might not abide by any court decision that didn't go his way. Blood might still run in the streets of Palmerton.

But not, Longarm vowed, if he had anything to say about it.

Chapter 9

"I was plannin' on takin' you over to Lariat after we'd paid a visit to the McCabe place," Walcott said as they rode back down the valley, "but I don't reckon we'd get a very friendly welcome there today."

Longarm smiled. "Might even get ourselves shot," he agreed.

They rode along in companionable silence for a few minutes, then Longarm saw a flash off to the right as sunlight reflected on metal. Alarm bells went off in his brain, and his instincts, honed by long years as a lawman, were about to fling him out of the saddle and make him yell for Walcott to get down. Then, even as Longarm's muscles tensed for action, he spotted a rider emerging from some trees and cantering toward the trail. He relaxed a little. The reflection could have come from the horse's harness or something else on the rider.

Walcott reined in. "Who's that comin'?" he asked.

"You'd know better than I would," Longarm pointed out. "This is your bailiwick, not mine."

They sat in the trail and waited as the rider approached, changing course slightly so as to come directly toward them. A moment later when sunlight flashed again, this time on long blonde hair, Longarm realized the horsebacker was a woman.

She lifted a hand in greeting as she reined in and called in a musical voice, "Hello, Sheriff!"

Walcott tugged on his hat brim. "Miss Mercedes. I thought that was you, but I wasn't sure till just now. Are you ridin' out here by yourself?"

"Is there any reason why I should not?"

"Well . . . that *is* McCabe range on that side of the trail."

The young woman called Mercedes shook her head. "I have no part in any silly feud. That is all my father's doing."

Longarm stiffened in the saddle. "Your father is Don Alejandro Montoya?" he asked.

The woman looked coolly at him. "That is right. I am Mercedes Montoya. But now you have the advantage on me, señor."

Longarm ticked a fingertip against the brim of his Stetson. "Custis Long," he introduced himself. "U.S. deputy marshal out of Denver."

"Sent down here to keep my father and Señora McCabe from killing each other, no doubt."

"Something like that," Longarm admitted.

"Good luck. My father is one of the stubbornest men on the face of the earth, especially when he thinks he has been wronged."

"The judge'll sort it all out next week," said Walcott. Mercedes Montoya gave him a look that said while she hoped that was true, she had her doubts.

One thing Longarm didn't have any doubts about was that this valley was full of good-looking women. First he'd encountered Estellita Rafferty, then Emily McCabe, and now Mercedes Montoya. Dressed in a dark riding skirt, a white blouse with a brown leather vest over it, and a flat-crowned black hat on her shining blonde hair, Mercedes was undeniably lovely.

"Your mother was Catalonian, wasn't she, ma'am?" asked Longarm, surprising Mercedes.

"Why, yes, she was. An aristocrat. She never really got used to this country after Papa brought her here from Spain. A shame, because I grew up here and I know its beauty."

Longarm figured she was three or four years older than Emily McCabe. The fellas in this part of the country must have been eagerly waiting for those two to grow up, he thought. There was nothing like a pretty girl to make a cowboy start thinking of moonlight and soft kisses. But Emily had wound up married to Tom McCabe, and Mercedes evidently wasn't married at all. There was no ring on her finger.

"You might ought to head back to Lariat, Miss Mercedes," Walcott said. "There was some trouble earlier today, and the country's sort of on edge."

"What happened?" Mercedes asked. "What has my father done now?"

"Nothin' really. He just rode over to the Box MCC with about twenty gun-totin' vaqueros." Quickly, Walcott explained about the battle he and Longarm had interrupted and how they had taken the wounded vaquero and his companions to the McCabe ranch.

"Dios mio!" exclaimed Mercedes. "That could have been bad, very bad."

"Yep, but cooler heads prevailed, as they say. Still, I reckon it'd be a good idea for you to go on home. Unless you were over here for a reason . . ."

Mercedes shook her head. "I was just out riding. I will take your advice, Sheriff." She looked at Longarm. "*Adios*, Marshal. I'm sure I will see you in town once the trial begins."

Longarm tipped his hat. "Yes, ma'am, I expect you will."

Mercedes turned her horse and rode off to the east, leaving the trail and cutting across country. From the confident way in which she rode, she knew exactly where she was going. Since she had grown up in these parts, she probably knew just about every square foot of the valley.

Longarm watched her go and then said, "I didn't know Montoya had a daughter."

"No reason you should have. Like she said, she steers clear of her father's ruckuses."

"Pretty girl."

"Yep. She's the spittin' image of her mama. Don't reckon Mercedes ever really knew her, though. Señora Montoya passed on when Mercedes was just a toddler."

The two lawmen jogged their horses into motion again and continued riding south toward Palmerton. "Emily McCabe's parents both died when she was young, too. I reckon you were acquainted with them?" Longarm asked after a few minutes.

"Oh, sure," said Walcott. "Jeff and Nora Griffith. Fine folks. Jeff was one of the first hands to sign on with Tom McCabe after he started the Box MCC. Nora's pa ran the freight line that came into Palmerton in those days. Nobody was surprised when they got hitched and Nora went to work cookin' on the McCabe ranch. Jeff moved out of the bunk house, of course. They had a little cabin of their own. A few years later, Emily came along, and I reckon they were sure happy for a couple of years until Nora took sick and died. After that, Tom hired a Mexican woman named Rosaria Canales to be the cook, and she became the closest thing Emily had to a mama, just like Tom was really the only papa she ever knew."

"And yet Emily grew up and married McCabe."

Walcott looked over narrowly at Longarm. "Don't go tryin' to make somethin' out of that," he said. "Like I told Emily, some folks thought Tom was an old goat and ought to be ashamed of himself for robbin' the cradle like that, and other folks probably figured Emily was just tryin' to latch on to a rich husband, but from everything I saw, those two really loved each other. And it ain't nobody else's business but theirs."

"Unless Emily had something to do with McCabe's death," Longarm said bluntly.

Walcott reined in and turned in the saddle to glare at Longarm. "Damn it, that just ain't possible!"

"I'm not saying it is. Just wondering."

"Well, you can stop wonderin'."

"Emily owns the McCabe ranch now. McCabe could've intended to leave it to his brother, and then Emily talked him into changing his will."

Walcott shook his head stubbornly. "No, sir, that ain't the way it was. Ask Ross Thayer if you want. He was Tom's lawyer, and he'll tell you Tom never intended to leave the ranch to Warren. Tom knew Warren couldn't handle the responsibility."

Longarm shrugged. "It's my job to poke around under all the rocks I can find."

"Well, you can just leave that rock alone, 'cause there ain't nothin' under it." Still in a huff, Walcott got his horse moving again.

Longarm rode alongside the sheriff without saying anything else. Since arriving in Palmerton nearly twenty-four hours before, he had met quite a few people and learned a great deal about the history of the valley, not to mention the romping he had done with Estellita Rafferty. He had even shot a fella in the arm. It was no wonder he was getting tired again. Longarm looked forward to arriving back in Palmerton. He wanted some supper, maybe a few drinks, and some sound sleep. That would help him sort everything out in his mind. As much fun as he'd had with Lita, it would be all right with him if she didn't come sneaking into his hotel room tonight.

The sun wasn't far above the mountain range to the west when Longarm and Walcott passed a smaller trail that veered off the northwest. Longarm had noticed it that morning when he and Walcott passed it the first time, but the sheriff hadn't mentioned it. Now Longarm said, "That must lead to the Diamond K. That's the name of Sam Kingston's spread, ain't it?"

"That's right," replied Walcott. "And if I ain't mistaken, that's Kingston and some of his boys coming toward us now."

Longarm saw the half-dozen riders coming up the trail from Palmerton. He and Walcott moved their horses to the side of the path so that the men could ride past. Instead, the man who seemed to be leading the group reined in, and the others followed suit. The leader was a big, raw-boned, downright ugly man wearing a high-crowned hat with a Montana pinch in it. In a harsh, high-pitched voice, he said. "Howdy, Sheriff. You out chasin' outlaws?"

"Nope, Sam, just visitin'," Walcott replied. "This here is Deputy Marshal Custis Long, from Denver."

"Federal man, eh?" Sam Kingston edged his horse closer and extended a hand to Longarm. "Pleased to meet you, Marshal. Kingston's my handle. Put Sam in front of it."

"Mr. Kingston," Longarm said with a nod as he shook the rancher's hand.

He had already spotted Nash Lundy among Kingston's men. The gunfighter wore his customary sardonic smile.

Longarm glanced at the other riders. They were about what he expected after seeing Lundy's companions the previous evening and hearing Walcott talk about how Kingston's crew was filled with gunmen. Lean, hard-featured men in range clothes, with rifles in their saddle boots and pistols on their hips. One of them even looked a little familiar to Longarm—

That was the one who, a second after Longarm looked at him, yelled, "Son of a bitch!" and grabbed for his gun.

Chapter 10

Longarm's hand flashed across his body and palmed the Colt from its holster. He didn't have to think about what he was doing. Muscles and nerves obeyed the impulses that his instincts sent screaming into his brain.

The gunman cleared leather, but just barely. In an eyeblink of time, Longarm had drawn his gun, and it blasted loudly, shattering the peaceful late-afternoon air. The gunman grunted and rocked back in the saddle as Longarm's bullet thudded into his chest, obliterating the paper tag hanging from a string attached to the pouch of tobacco in his breast pocket. The gunman's unfired pistol slipped from his nerveless fingers and fell onto the trail, followed a second later by its owner's body as the man swayed and pitched out of the saddle.

The shooting was over so quickly that no one else had had a chance to move.

Then, with snarled curses, several of Kingston's men reached for their guns. "Hold it!" Kingston and Walcott shouted at the same time. Walcott went on, "The next fella who pulls a gun'll either die for it right here or hang for it later."

"No shootin'!" bellowed Kingston. "Nash, I'm talkin' to you, damn it!"

Lundy had come closer than any of the others to getting his gun out. His hand was on the butt of the weapon. He was still smiling as he leaned forward a little in his saddle, but his eyes reminded Longarm of a rattlesnake's eyes—cold and deadly and almost inhuman. A faint tremor went through Lundy, and he wrenched his hand away from his gun.

A thin spiral of smoke still drifted from the barrel of Longarm's Colt. He lowered the weapon and said to the rancher, "Your man didn't give me any choice, Kingston. You all saw him go for his gun first."

"Yeah," Kingston admitted, "but why in blazes did he do that?"

Longarm thought hard, and he was able to put a name with the face that had been vaguely familiar. "Because I recognized him," he said. "His name was Dave Parnell."

Lundy said angrily, "His name was Dan Porter. You've got the wrong man, Marshal."

Longarm shook his head. "He called himself Parnell when he was part of a gang up in Wyoming last year holding up stagecoaches and murdering the drivers. I rounded up all the rest of the bunch, but Parnell got away. Reckon he must've drifted down here, and when he saw me he figured I'd tracked him down and aimed to take him in."

Walcott said, "Porter's only been ridin' for you about six months, ain't that right, Sam?"

Grudgingly, Kingston nodded. "Yeah. And I didn't know him before then, so I reckon he could be that Parnell feller the marshal's talking about."

"That's no reason to gun him down," snapped Nash Lundy.

"Dan went for his gun first," Kingston said with a sigh. "I don't reckon we can hold it against the marshal that he defended hisself."

Longarm finally slid his revolver back into its holster. The threat of impending violence that had filled the air a few moments earlier had seeped away. Kingston's men were still pretty edgy, and Nash Lundy looked like he would have gladly put a bullet in Longarm—or tried to, anyway—but Longarm didn't think anything else was going to happen. Not when Kingston had given specific orders to the contrary.

Kingston jerked a thumb toward the trail that led to the Diamond K. "You boys go on back to the spread," he said. "I'll be there later. Before you go, though, throw Dan's body over his saddle. I'll tote him back to the undertaker's place in town."

"I can do that for you if you want, Sam," Walcott offered.

Kingston shook his head as a couple of his men dismounted and tied Parnell across the saddle on the back of the dead man's nervous horse. "No, it's my job to do," he said.

"Well, I'm sorry it had to happen."

Kingston looked at Longarm. "I am, too."

Longarm didn't say anything. He sat there, hands crossed on his saddlehorn, until Kingston had started back to Palmerton with the corpse and the other men had ridden on toward the Diamond K.

Walcott shook his head. "You seem to have a knack for makin' enemies, Marshal. Montoya's probably still mad at you for ventilatin' that vaquero o' his, and now you got Nash Lundy lookin' at you like he wishes it was over a gunsight."

"You seem to be a pretty good judge of character, Sheriff. Is Lundy the sort to ambush a fella?"

"I don't know what Lundy's capable of," Walcott said flatly. "And I don't reckon I want to find out. I'd keep a close eye on my back for a while if I was you, though."

"I always do," said Longarm.

Nothing else happened on the way back into town, and Longarm was profoundly grateful for that. He could understand why Billy Vail had sent him down here. This valley was a powderkeg ready to blow, and it wouldn't take much of a spark to set it off. Open war could break out between the men of the Box MCC and the vaqueros from Lariat, and if it did, Longarm was confident that Sam Kingston and his gunnies would be waiting to swoop in and clean up the leavings for themselves.

Longarm and Walcott parted company in front of the Valley Hotel. Before riding back to the sheriff's office, Walcott asked, "Think we can keep the lid on until next Tuesday?"

"Maybe," Longarm said. "But just because the trial starts there's no guarantee things won't still boil over."

Walcott sighed. "I know. Well, like the old hymn says, further along we'll know more about it."

Longarm frowned. That was an old saying *he* liked to use. He rubbed his jaw and said, "Yep. You can only eat an apple one bite at a time, I reckon."

Walcott's eyes narrowed. "Uh-huh," he said. "Be seein' you." He turned his horse and rode off.

Longarm took the steeldust to the corral behind the hotel and grained and watered the horse, then went into the building through the back door. He met Mrs. Cochran on his way to the stairs. "Oh, Mr. Long," she said, "a telegram came for you. It's at the desk. I'll get it."

Longarm went with her into the lobby and took the yellow telegraph flimsy from her. It was folded, but she could have opened it and read it. Longarm did so now and saw that it was from Billy Vail, asking for a report from him. It hadn't taken long for Billy to get impatient, Longarm thought. But Vail would just have to wait. Other than closing the books on the stagecoach robber and killer Dave Parnell, Longarm hadn't really accomplished much since arriving in the valley.

He nodded to Mrs. Cochran and said, "Thanks."

"If you need to send a reply, the Western Union office is closed by now, but Mr. Hawley, the telegrapher, lives right upstairs from it. You could go up and knock on his door."

Longarm shook his head. "No need to disturb him." He tucked the flimsy into his shirt pocket and headed for the stairs.

When he reached his room, he looked down. The matchstick he had carefully positioned between the door and the jamb when he left the room that morning was still in place. No one had been inside. He unlocked the door and went in.

Just as he had thought, nothing was disturbed. He tossed his hat on the bed. The room was fairly dim, since twilight was settling down over the town and the curtains were closed, cutting off most of the light that was left. Longarm took a lucifer from his pocket and went to light the lamp.

The flame had just taken good hold on the wick when window glass tinkled and the lamp exploded. Longarm threw himself backward and fell heavily to the floor. The kerosene in the lamp's reservoir splashed over the table and caught fire with a *whoosh* of flames. The blaze licked hungrily across the floor toward Longarm, following some of the spilled kerosene.

He scrambled away from the fire and leaped to his feet. The room was filled now with flickering light from the kerosene-fueled conflagration. Longarm lunged toward the window, intending to rip down the curtains and use them to beat out the flames, then remembered almost too late what had started the fire in the first place. He jerked his body aside.

Something whipped past his ear as more glass shattered. Longarm dove for the floor. If he pulled the curtains down, he would be visible to the bushwhacker whose first shot had broken the lamp and who was still slinging lead into the room. He heard a third bullet thud into the wall next to the door.

If he didn't do something about the fire, though, he might burn to death, because the flames were already between him and the door. Not to mention the fact that the whole hotel might burn down. Coughing as smoke began to fill the room, Longarm reached over and dragged the bedspread off the bed.

He stood up, trying to stay out of a direct line with the window, and began beating at the flames with the bedspread. He wasn't sure that was going to do the job, but it was the only option he had. The fierce heat from the blaze washed over him and almost drove him back, but he forced himself to keep swinging the bedspread.

Shouts came from elsewhere in the hotel. People had surely smelled the smoke by now and knew a fire was burning somewhere. That meant help was on the way and would soon be here. But anyone who came in to help him fight the fire ran the risk of falling victim to a bushwhacker's bullet.

Something tugged at the sleeve of Longarm's shirt. Another slug from the bushwhacker's gun, he thought. He was getting damned sick and tired of this. How was a fella supposed to put out a fire when he had to worry about getting shot?

Longarm dropped the bedspread, which was pretty charred by now, and went to his knees. He crawled across the room to the window and reached up to grasp the curtains. Shards of glass from the broken window lay on the floor, and as they cut into his knees, it just made him angrier. With a savage tug, he yanked the curtains down.

Orange muzzle flame winked from the roof of a building

across the street. An unbroken pane of glass exploded and showered down on Longarm's shoulders as he hunched his head forward. He drew his gun, jabbed the barrel through a hole in the window, and started firing toward the spot where he had seen the muzzle flash.

He emptied the Colt in a long roll of thundering shots, then dropped back out of the window. The fire was still burning, but he hoped that his volley would spook the ambusher and buy him a few moments. He snatched up the curtains and started slapping at the flames again.

The door of the room burst open, and Mrs. Cochran came running in with a bucket of water in her hands. She flung the water on the fire, then handed the empty bucket to a man in the hall. A moment later, another bucket was passed forward and dumped on the flames. Obviously, Mrs. Cochran had already organized a bucket brigade from the pump downstairs. She wasn't going to let her hotel burn up without a fight.

Longarm kept up his efforts with the curtains, throwing a glance at the broken window every now and then. He didn't see any more muzzle flashes from across the street, and he didn't hear any more bullets whipping past his head. Maybe he had actually hit the bushwhacker, he thought, even though his intention had been just to distract the murderous bastard. Or the rifleman might have seen that there were now innocent people in the room, and he had decided not to risk killing one of them with a stray bullet. Longarm didn't really care which possibility was right. He just hoped the son of a bitch wouldn't start shooting again.

His arms were mighty tired from swinging the curtains by the time the fire was finally out. The stench of smoke filled his nostrils and permeated his clothes. It would take some scrubbing to get rid of it. But although half the floor, one entire wall, and most of the ceiling were badly burned, at least the danger of the whole hotel going up in flames had been averted.

"My Lord!" Mrs. Cochran said. Her gray hair hung in her face, and her dress was soaked from the water that had sloshed out of the buckets. "What happened, Mr. Long?"

Longarm gestured toward the bullet-riddled window.

"Somebody started taking potshots at me. The first one happened to bust the lamp and start the fire."

The woman stared at him, aghast. "But why would anyone want to do that?"

Longarm didn't reply. Even though he had only been in Palmerton for a day, there were already too many answers to choose from when the question was who might want him dead.

Chapter 11

Mrs. Cochran was a little leery of allowing Longarm to remain in the hotel, but she was too good a hostess to kick him out. As he gathered up his gear to move to another room, this one on the ground floor, she looked around at the damage and said, "I'll get the carpenters in here first thing tomorrow to start repairing all this."

"I'm mighty sorry it happened, ma'am," Longarm told her as he put on his hat. The Stetson stunk of smoke, too, just like the rest of his clothes. "If you'd like, you can send a claim for the damages to Chief Marshal Vail in Denver. I ain't saying it'll do any good, but it can't hurt to try. I'll sure tell him what happened."

"Thank you, Mr. Long. I'll do that." She wrinkled her nose. "In the meantime, I fear that you'll have to do something about those clothes of yours. They're covered with soot and they really don't smell very good."

"Yes, ma'am. You have a laundry here in town?"

"We do. If you'll leave your things in the hall outside your new room, I'll have a boy take them over and get them washed."

"I'll be much obliged to you for your kindness," Longarm said honestly. He carried his Winchester and saddlebags downstairs and into the room she showed him, which was smaller and tucked away underneath the stairs. There was no window in this room, but after what had happened, Longarm didn't really care about that. It might get a little stuffy, but at least folks couldn't shoot at him as easily.

When he was alone, he undressed down to the buff and opened the door just long enough to pile the clothes on the floor. His boots and hat smelled of smoke, too, but there was nothing he could do about that. For that matter, so did he. First thing in the morning, he decided, he would go over to the barbershop and wash up. He had seen a sign out in front of the place advertising baths for two bits.

He had just stretched out naked on the bed when he realized that with everything that was going on, he had plumb forgotten to eat supper. His stomach growled at him. He had a clean shirt and a clean bottom half to a set of long underwear in his saddlebag, and closed up as they had been, they probably didn't stink too badly. But he couldn't go out wearing just a shirt and underwear, and he didn't want to bother Mrs. Cochran any more, so he told himself he'd just have to wait until breakfast. It wouldn't be the first time in his life he had gone to sleep hungry.

He rolled over and tried to distract himself by thinking about the ambush attempt. That hot-headed Chuy Valdez could have been the bushwhacker, he thought, or another of Montoya's vaqueros who wanted revenge for what had happened to Lupe. An even more likely suspect was Nash Lundy, or one of Kingston's other gunmen. There were plenty of possibilities to choose from.

And what had happened with Dave Parnell was a perfect example of a burden Longarm always had to bear, too. He had been a lawman for a long time, and there were dozens, maybe even hundreds, of people in the world who carried a grudge against him. Folks he had arrested or tried to arrest, sons and brothers and fathers of men he had killed in the line of duty, criminals whose schemes he had ruined. Longarm sighed. The list was mighty nigh endless, and he always risked running into one of them by sheer chance. The ambush might not have any connection with the job he'd been sent here to do.

Longarm was turning all that over in his mind when he finally dozed off.

• • •

Despite being hungry, he slept soundly, and he didn't wake up until he heard the faint click of a key in the lock the next morning.

He was instantly alert, but he didn't reach for his gun. He lay there on his back, his eyes slitted, as the door swung open and Estellita Rafferty stepped into the room. She had a bundle of clean clothes in her arms. She set them quietly on the room's single chair. In the light that came in from the hallway, Longarm watched her. She looked mighty pretty this morning in a low-cut white blouse and a dark blue skirt. She started to turn back toward the door, but she stopped and looked at him lying in bed. He didn't figure she could tell he was awake.

A moment later he was sure of it, because she lifted her hands to her breasts and cupped them. She began squeezing and caressing herself. Longarm wondered if she was remembering all the things they had done together a couple of nights before. She must have been, because she slipped her right hand under the waistband of her skirt and started rubbing herself. Longarm felt bad about letting her think he was asleep while she put on such a display.

She didn't think that for long, however, because a moment later she stopped what she was doing and jerked her hand out of her crotch. "You . . . you terrible man!" she gasped. "You are awake!"

Longarm couldn't help but chuckle. "How'd you know, Lita?"

She pointed accusingly.

Longarm lifted his head from the pillow and looked down at his middle. The sheet was tented up dramatically over the throbbing erection she had given him. Longarm grinned and shrugged.

Lita stepped over beside the bed. "You watched me, now I will watch you." Before he could stop her, she reached down and grabbed the sheet, flinging it back so that his hard shaft was exposed.

Longarm scrambled up into a sitting position. "Dadgum it, the door's open!" he said. "Mrs. Cochran or anybody else could walk by."

Lita curled her fingers around his manhood. "Are you saying you want me to leave?" she asked with a smile.

"Hell, no. Just close the door."

She let go of him and stepped over to the door. When she had closed it, enough light still came through the small gaps around it for him to be able to see her as she peeled off her blouse and skirt. She was naked underneath them.

She climbed onto the bed and straddled his hips. "Fast now," she said. "Then again, slow." She grasped his shaft and lowered herself onto it.

Longarm gave her what she wanted, sheathing himself in her and grasping her hips so that he could help her pump them up and down rapidly. Lita bent her head and kissed him, panting into his mouth as her excitement grew. After only a few moments, Longarm plunged as deeply within her as he could and began to spasm. His seed welled out and filled her heated chamber, mingling with her own juices to coat them both.

With his heart thudding heavily in his chest and his pulse pounding in his head, Longarm lay back and tried to catch his breath. His manhood stayed where it was, buried deeply inside Lita. When he started to withdraw, she clenched her muscles around him. "Stay in me," she whispered.

Longarm decided he could do that. He toyed with Lita's heavy breasts, tugging gently on the hard nipples. Her fingers explored the forest of dark brown hair on his chest. After a time she leaned back so that she could reach behind her and feel the place where they were still joined. She played with his sacs, cupping them and rolling them back and forth in her palm. Longarm's organ had softened, but just a little. He was still surprisingly hard.

He got an even bigger surprise when Lita stretched out both legs and lifted her knees, then turned around so that she was facing away from him, all the while remaining impaled on the spike of his manhood. She lay down on his thighs, and when he raised his head he could see the base of his shaft where it was imbedded between her feminine folds. Right above it was the cleft of her buttocks, opened wide so that the puckered ring of that orifice was plainly visible.

Lita began working her hips back and forth so that he could see himself sliding in and out of her. He was fully erect again now. In a voice husky with passion, she pleaded, "Put your finger in my bottom."

Longarm scooped up a dollop of the cream that had overflowed from their first lovemaking and used it for lubrication as he slipped the middle finger of his right hand up her tight rear passage. Lita went wild and would have galloped to the finish, but Longarm remembered her saying that she wanted this time to be slow. He held her hip with his other hand and said, "Not yet."

Lita moaned. She was leaning over and had hold of his ankles to brace herself as she rode him. Longarm began thrusting slowly in and out of her, at the same time pushing his finger into her and then withdrawing it part of the way. She gasped, "Oh, Custis, you're filling me up!"

He made it last as long as he could, but he wasn't made of iron. Eventually he felt his own climax building up again. He pushed his finger into her bottom as far as it would go and began rotating it carefully. Lita bucked back against him and began to shudder. He came with her, his organ jerking as his seed gouted from it once again.

Feeling as if his heart were going to burst right out of his chest, Longarm fell back against the headboard of the bed. Lita collapsed in the other direction, across his legs. This time when he withdrew from her, she made no complaint. She probably knew, like he did, that if they attempted anything else right now, it would likely kill both of them.

After a few minutes, Lita turned around and snuggled up beside him. "That was the best, Custis," she said. "The best I've ever had."

He chuckled wearily. "As young as you are, gal, that can't have been too much."

She licked his left nipple. "You'd be surprised. The boys around here think I'm just a tease, but when I come across a real man like you— By the way, you smell like smoke, and you taste a little like it, too."

"I plan on taking a bath this morning," he told her. "You just got to me first. Thanks for bringing back my clothes. I didn't know you were the town laundress."

"I'm not. But I heard about what happened last night at the hotel—I think the whole town has heard—and when I saw old Mrs. Ramirez coming out of her place with your clothes, I recognized them and knew she must have washed them. I offered to deliver them for her."

"You delivered more than clothes," said Longarm.

She giggled. "And aren't you glad that I did?"

He squeezed her with the arm he had around her shoulders. "Yeah, but right now I could use some breakfast."

She pouted a little at that, but Longarm didn't think she was serious. She slipped out of bed and reached for her skirt. "Come back to the cantina with me," she said. "I will make breakfast for you."

"That's the best offer—no, the second-best offer—I've had so far this morning."

"But when you are finished—" She pulled her blouse over her head and shook her hair back into place. "You really do have to go to the barber's and get that bath."

Chapter 12

Sheriff Walcott stopped by Longarm's table in the cantina while he was eating breakfast. Longarm was alone, Lita having gone back into the kitchen after delivering his plate of scrambled eggs, peppers, beans, and tortillas.

"Heard all the shootin' last night," the sheriff said as he reversed one of the chairs and straddled it. "Time I pulled my pants on and got down to the hotel, though, it was all over. You'd already moved to another room and Miz Cochran said you wasn't to be disturbed. I wasn't just about to argue with her."

"You're scared of that sweet little old lady, Sheriff?"

"Huh!" Walcott grunted explosively. "Sweet little old lady, my foot. When she gets her dander up, she's a holy terror. But she's a handsome woman for a widow lady." Walcott grinned. "I been thinkin' about courtin' her. I'll be ready to hang up my badge and gun in another year or two, and she's got that nice, money-makin' hotel—"

"I don't want to take your mind off the future," Longarm said, "but we still got some problems right here in the present, old son. Somebody did their damnedest to kill me last night."

Walcott grew solemn and nodded. "Once Miz Cochran told me the bushwhacker's first shot busted the lamp in your room and started the fire, I figured the bastard must've been on the roof of the building across the street."

"That's where he was, all right," Longarm said. "I saw his muzzle flashes and threw a little lead his way."

"Well, you didn't do anything but put some holes in the false front of the hardware store. I took a lantern over there and had a look around. Found a few tracks in the alley around a ladder, but that don't necessarily mean anything. Lots of folks go up and down the alleys in this town. No blood to be seen anywhere, either in the alley or on the roof."

"What about shell casings?"

Walcott shook his head. "Nope. Nary a one. Whoever the bushwhacker was, he picked up after himself."

"Got any ideas about who it might've been?"

"First one that comes to mind is Nash Lundy," Walcott said heavily. "You'd play hob provin' it, though. Ever' other hand on Kingston's spread would swear Lundy never left the place last night."

Longarm nodded. "That's just what I figured. Could have been one of Montoya's men, too. Like that Chuy Valdez."

"Valdez still don't seem the type to me," Walcott said with a shrug, "but I reckon we can't rule out anybody just yet." The local lawman leaned forward and lowered his voice. "Say, Emiliano ain't lookin' too friendly this mornin' when he glances over thisaway. What's his problem?"

"You heard Montoya say yesterday that him and Rafferty are old friends. I reckon he's heard about what happened out at the McCabe ranch."

"Could be." Walcott gestured at the remains of Longarm's breakfast. "See he don't mind feedin' you, though."

"That was Lita's doing," Longarm said as he picked up his coffee cup to down the last of the strong black brew.

"Didn't I warn you about that little gal? She'll act like she's sweet on you, but you'll be disappointed if you get your hopes up."

Longarm just smiled to himself. He didn't want to disillusion the sheriff, but he wasn't disappointed a bit in Lita Rafferty. Far from it, in fact. He was downright impressed.

"Still three days until the trial starts," Walcott went on. "What do you figure on doin' between now and then?"

Longarm leaned back in his chair and took out a cheroot. He put it in his mouth unlit and said, "Tom McCabe's murder interests me."

"Murder ain't a federal crime," Walcott pointed out.

"No, and I ain't trying to step on your toes, Sheriff. But I figure it might help to keep things under control now if I knew how they got this way. I reckon you investigated when McCabe was ambushed."

"Of course I did. Took a posse and rode over damned near every foot of the Box MCC. Found some hoofprints on a ridge that overlooked the place where Tom was shot, but the ground was so rocky there wasn't a trail to follow." Walcott tugged on his mustache and frowned in thought. "No shell casin's up there, neither. Just like on the roof of the hardware store after whoever it was tried for you."

"If you had murdered one of the most powerful men in the territory, you might get a little nervous if a federal lawman came in and started poking around," Longarm said.

"Yeah. Son of a bitch probably figures I ain't no threat to him." Walcott sounded angry.

Longarm did his best not to smile. "Don't get your fur in an uproar, Sheriff. The killer would probably feel the same way if you were to open up the case again."

Walcott slapped a palm down on the table. "Dadblast it, that's just what I'm goin' to do!" he declared. "I gave up too damned easy."

"Hold on." Longarm lifted a hand in a calming gesture. "I'd rather you let me nose around a mite on my own. For one thing, you're needed here in town to make sure things stay peaceful until the trial starts."

"Well, yeah, I reckon so," Walcott said grudgingly. "All right. I won't get in your way, Marshal. But if you come up with anything, I'd sure appreciate knowin' about it."

"You'll be the first one I tell," promised Longarm. "Now, you reckon you can tell me how to get to the place where Warren McCabe found his brother's body?"

Longarm walked the steeldust along the faint, narrow game trail. It wound through the rolling hills of the Box MCC, and according to Sheriff Walcott, Tom McCabe had been riding this trail on the day he was ambushed and killed. Longarm had found the path easily enough following Walcott's directions. He had not gone by the ranch house, preferring not to announce his presence.

He came to a place where the ground abruptly shelved off to the right of the trail and reined in. At the bottom of the thirty-foot drop was a scattering of boulders. According to Walcott, the fatal shot had struck McCabe in the back while he was riding along here and dumped him out of his saddle to plunge down into those rocks. If the bullet hadn't killed him, the fall might have, thought Longarm, but Walcott had been pretty definite that McCabe had died almost instantly from the wound.

Longarm hipped around in the saddle and studied his surroundings. Ahead of him, the trail followed the rimrock for a little way, then twisted off to the west into a rugged area cut by several ravines. To the east and south were rolling hills, good grazing range for the ranch's stock. To the southwest another ridge rose so that it overlooked the trail where Longarm sat on the steeldust.

That ridge was the only good place for a bushwhacker to wait for Tom McCabe, Longarm decided. He turned the horse toward it and looked for a way up. It took him several minutes to find a slope that was gentle enough for the steeldust to negotiate.

As he rode up toward the top of the other ridge, a deer burst out of a nearby clump of trees. Longarm reined in for a moment and watched in admiration as the wild animal bounded away, its muscles working smoothly under its sleek hide. He hadn't had time to count the points on its antlers, but they would have made a good trophy for Sheriff Walcott, who, judging by the display in his office, was quite proud of his hunting prowess.

Longarm rode on and a few minutes later emerged on the rim of the higher ridge. He reined in sharply when he saw a figure sitting there on horseback.

Emily McCabe was staring out across the valley, and at first she seemed not to notice Longarm's arrival. Then she took a deep breath and turned the chestnut mare she was riding so that she was facing him as he came toward her.

As he reined in, Longarm reached up to tug on the brim of his hat. "Mrs. McCabe," he greeted her.

"Marshal." She rode astride, wearing a man's shirt and denim trousers that tightly hugged her thighs. A floppy-brimmed black hat was on her head. Her raven-dark hair had been done into two long braids that lay on her shoulders. At first glance she looked about sixteen years old. You had to look at her eyes and see the pain there to realize she was a grown woman, with a grown woman's problems.

"Didn't expect to run into you out here," Longarm said. "Hope you don't take offense that I'm riding your range without letting you know."

She shook her head. "Of course not. Are you looking for anything in particular?"

Longarm hesitated, then decided to be blunt. She had to know what had happened here just as well as he did. "I was taking a look at the place where your husband was killed," he said.

Emily nodded. "So was I. I come out here every now and then . . . probably too often . . . because this was the last place where Tom was alive. That's the way I prefer to think of it." She lifted a hand and pointed. "Even from the lower ridge where Tom was riding, you can see a long way across the valley. That's why he came up here, to look out over the land and see what he had made of it. He was proud. He was a very proud man—"

Her voice broke, and her face crumpled into tears. She lifted her hands and covered her face. Longarm sat quietly on the steeldust, a little embarrassed to be here right now.

After a few moments, Emily wiped the sleeve of her shirt across her eyes and managed a faint smile. "I'm sorry, Marshal," she said. "It's been long enough now that I don't normally break down like that very often. But Tom's death still hurts a great deal."

"Yes, ma'am, I'm sure it does."

"I probably shouldn't torture myself by coming up here. Sometimes I just can't help it."

She was either a better actress than Lily Langtry and Sarah Bernhardt combined, Longarm thought, or she had really loved her husband and was still mourning him. He didn't figure she was that good an actress. It was probably time to forget about any lingering suspicions he might have had that she could be involved in McCabe's murder.

"You must have thought about it," Longarm said. "Who do you think could have bushwhacked your husband?"

Emily's lips tightened into a grim line. "Montoya," she

said without hesitation. "He knew he was going to lose his ridiculous lawsuit."

"Sheriff Walcott says Montoya isn't a backshooter."

"Then he had one of his men do it," Emily snapped.

"What about Sam Kingston?"

The question seemed to take Emily by surprise. "What about him?"

"I hear that he wouldn't mind getting his hands on the Box MCC. Maybe he figured that with your husband gone, he could move in and grab the ranch from you and your brother-in-law."

Emily shrugged. "I don't think Sam Kingston is any more honest than he has to be. I suppose he could have had something to do with Tom's death."

"Seems just as likely to me as Montoya."

"Maybe." Clearly, Emily disliked Montoya to the point that she would have been willing to blame him for just about anything that went wrong on the McCabe spread.

"Can you think of anybody else?"

Emily shook her head. "No, I'm sorry, Marshal, I can't."

"I've been told that Tom McCabe was a hard man. Hard men usually have plenty of enemies."

"Some people probably resented his success, and a few may have thought he took advantage of them in business dealings, but Tom was always scrupulously fair and honest. No one hated him enough to kill him except Montoya. Or maybe Kingston," she added as an afterthought.

Longarm changed the subject by saying, "What about that lawsuit? You think your husband would have won?"

"Of course. Montoya has no proof that the original land grant extended onto this side of the valley."

"What if he had the grant document itself?"

"That's been lost for decades," Emily said. "That's why Montoya didn't win years ago when he first challenged Tom's claim to the Box MCC. The land commissioner who came out from Washington said that without the document, Montoya didn't have a case. I don't know why he ever brought it up again."

"Maybe now he has the document," Longarm suggested. "Sometimes things that are lost don't stay that way. It could have turned up."

Emily's eyes widened. Obviously, she had never considered that possibility. "You really think so?"

"I don't know. But it'd go a long way toward clearing things up if I could get a look at that document."

"That's impossible," Emily said, but she didn't sound completely convinced now. "Surely it's still lost."

"Maybe I ought to ride over to Montoya's and ask him."

"They might shoot you on sight," Emily warned.

Longarm chuckled. "Killing a U.S. deputy marshal three days before you're going into a federal court ain't a very good way to win a case. I reckon Montoya will listen to reason, and I figure he can keep his men in line."

"Well, good luck." Emily turned the mare. "I'd better get back to the ranch house. Ross is coming for lunch."

Longarm nodded and tugged on his hat brim again. He sat there and watched Emily ride away. His visit to the McCabe spread really hadn't turned up anything new, but he was glad he had ridden out here anyway. He felt like he knew Emily McCabe better now. That might be important somewhere down the line.

For now, though, his next stop was Lariat, and he hoped he was right about Montoya and his men not trying to kill him.

Chapter 13

The Montoya hacienda, not surprisingly, was quite old. Longarm could tell that by looking at it as he rode up. A thick stone wall six feet high surrounded the main house. In the early days, when this was still part of New Spain, the wall would have been built to defend against Indians who didn't care for the Spanish intruders. Inside the wall, the big adobe house itself appeared to be equally sturdy. The windows were narrow, so that they could serve as rifle ports, and the roof was made of red clay tile that wouldn't burn in case attackers tried to use flaming arrows. Longarm assumed the house was constructed in the usual Spanish style and had a plaza in the center of it.

Now that the territory was semi-civilized and the threat of Indian attacks was pretty much gone, the ranch headquarters had expanded outside the wall. Longarm saw several barns and corrals, a long adobe building that was probably a bunk house, a smithy, and several other outbuildings. Like the Box MCC, Lariat could be largely self-sufficient if need be.

A barking dog announced that he was riding up. Several men came out of one of the barns to greet him, among them Chuy Valdez. When the young vaquero recognized Longarm, he moved his hand toward the butt of his gun. One of the other men spoke sharply to him in Spanish, and Valdez sullenly nodded. He took his hand away from his gun.

As Longarm reined in, the man who had spoken to Valdez

came up to him and said, "I am Esteban. What do you want here, Brazo Largo?" At Longarm's look of surprise, the man went on, "*Si*, I know what our people below the border call you, Señor Long."

Longarm rested his hands on the saddlehorn and asked, "Are you in charge around here today, Esteban?"

"I am Don Alejandro's *segundo*."

"Where is Don Alejandro?"

Esteban waved a callused hand toward the north. "He rides the range. Despite his years, he is not one to sit at home in his parlor and remember the days that once were."

"You expect him back any time soon?"

"Not until late this afternoon. But if there is anything I can do to help you—"

Longarm thought Esteban looked a little familiar. "You were at the McCabe place yesterday with Don Alejandro, weren't you?"

"*Si*. Of course."

"I'm a mite surprised you haven't taken a shotgun after me."

Esteban shook his head. "We are law-abiding people on this ranch, unlike those who ride for the McCabe brand. We wanted only to free our compadres from captivity."

"Well, I'm glad to hear it. The part about being law-abiding, I mean." Longarm didn't figure that Esteban could—or would—help him much in his investigation of the trouble in the valley, so he was about to make his farewells and ride off when a new voice spoke up.

"Marshal Long. So good to see you again."

Longarm turned his head and saw Mercedes Montoya standing in an open gate under a black wrought-iron arch in the stone wall around the hacienda. She wore a short-sleeved red and blue dress decorated with a lot of fancy embroidery and she looked lovely. Longarm tipped his hat to her and said, "Señorita Montoya."

"What can we do for you, Marshal?"

Longarm nodded toward Esteban. "I was just asking your segundo here a few questions. He tells me your father won't be back until later today."

"That is true. Papa loves to get out of the house and work

with the men. But I would be very pleased if you would come in and join me for lunch."

The invitation took Longarm by surprise. He glanced at Esteban and the other vaqueros and saw that they didn't look too happy about it, especially Chuy Valdez. The young puncher's eyes had narrowed down to cold, angry slits.

None of them were going to go against the daughter of their *patron*, however, and Longarm decided he wouldn't mind talking to Mercedes Montoya. "Much obliged for the invite," he said as he swung down from the steeldust. "It'll be my pleasure, ma'am."

"Excellent. Esteban, see to the marshal's horse, will you?"

"*Si*, señorita," Esteban replied as he reached out to take the reins from Longarm.

Valdez looked mad enough to chew nails, Longarm thought as he strolled over to the gate to join Mercedes. And it wasn't just because Longarm was a gringo, or a lawman, or anything else. Longarm knew jealousy when he saw it. Valdez was interested in Mercedes for himself.

Well, he was out of luck today, Longarm thought with a smile. Mercedes offered him her arm, and he took it. She led him through the gate and along a flagstone walk toward a thick wooden door in the hacienda itself.

"I am glad you stopped by today, Marshal," Mercedes said. "I get lonely here on the ranch. We so seldom get any company."

"Is that why you like to go riding?"

"I suppose. Although I enjoy being out of doors, just like my father. One of his legacies to me, I suppose."

Longarm wondered what other legacies Montoya might leave to her. As far as he knew, Mercedes was the old man's only child. When he was gone, she might inherit Lariat. On the other hand, the fact that she was a female could work against her. Montoya might leave the ranch to one of his male relatives down in Mexico.

But he was getting ahead of himself, Longarm realized. From what he had seen of Montoya, the man was still quite vital despite his age. Otherwise, why would he have asked Emily McCabe to marry him?

And Longarm wondered how that proposal had gone over with Mercedes?

"It's such a nice day we'll eat on the patio," Mercedes said as she led Longarm into the house and along a passage into the plaza in the center. It was a pretty place, open to the sky above but surrounded by the house. A balcony ran all the way around on the second floor. In the center of the plaza was a fountain with a low stone wall around it. A flagstone patio jutted out into the plaza, and Longarm saw a table and chairs on it. That was where Mercedes took him.

"Please sit down," she said. "I'll tell Conchita that there will be a guest for lunch."

Longarm sat down at the table and placed his hat on the flagstones beside his chair while Mercedes disappeared into the house for a few moments. When she came back, she carried a pitcher full of yellow liquid and a couple of glasses.

"Would you care for some lemonade? It is freshly made and chilled."

"That sounds mighty nice," said Longarm. "Thanks."

She poured the lemonade, then sat down across the table from him and sipped from her glass. Longarm followed suit and found the drink to be just the right mixture of sweet and tart, and its cool smoothness tasted good on this warm day.

"This is a mighty nice place," he commented. "The house is, what, a couple of hundred years old?"

"About that," said Mercedes. "I do not know the exact year it was built."

"The old land grant document would have a date on it, wouldn't it?"

Her full red lips curved in a smile. "You are fishing, Marshal. That document has been missing for years, as I'm sure you have been told."

"Missing things sometimes turn up," he said again, just as he had to Emily McCabe earlier today.

"Sometimes," Mercedes said cryptically.

Longarm didn't ask any more questions right then because a serving woman came out of the house carrying several platters of food. There were strips of beef and chicken, still sizzling from the pan where they had been cooked, along with beans and tortillas and red and green peppers and wild onions. The woman placed the food on the table, and Longarm and Mercedes began to eat.

It was good—maybe not quite as good as what Lita Rafferty dished up at the cantina in town, but tasty nonetheless. Longarm was still catching up after missing supper the night before, so he ate heartily.

Mercedes said, "My father and Chuy and the other men seem to regard you as an enemy, but you seem like a good man to me, Marshal Long."

"I try to be," Longarm said with a shrug. "But my job is to uphold the law and see that justice is done as much as possible, and sometimes that don't make a fella very many friends."

"Will it be justice if my father is denied the land that is rightfully his?"

"If he can prove it, I reckon the judge will decide in his favor. If he can't . . . well, that's just the way things work. The court has to go by the evidence."

"Of course," Mercedes said, but she sounded a little bitter. "An American court."

"Seems to me that if you're here and intend to stay here, you're an American, no matter where your family came from," Longarm pointed out.

"Perhaps, but my father will never agree with that. He is too proud."

Pride was something that wasn't in short supply in this valley, thought Longarm. Earlier today, Emily had been talking about what a proud man Tom McCabe had been, and now Mercedes spoke of her father in the same way.

Since Montoya wasn't here, maybe he could get a little more background from the man's daughter, Longarm decided. He took another sip of his lemonade and then asked, "Do you have any brothers or sisters?"

Mercedes shook her head. "No, I am the only child with which my mother and father were blessed. At least, I hope they considered me a blessing. With my mother, it was hard to tell."

Longarm knew Montoya was a widower, otherwise he couldn't have asked Emily to marry him, but he didn't know anything about Montoya's first wife. He said, "Your mother was a difficult woman?"

"My mother was insane," Mercedes said flatly. "By the time I was born she was already losing her mind. My father hoped that having the responsibility of a child would help her, but it seemed to drive her further into madness."

"I'm sorry," Longarm said.

"There was nothing anyone could do. Mama missed her homeland so much that she could never be happy living here. So she retreated into her own head, I suppose you could say. I remember as a young girl going into her room and asking her to brush my hair. She did not know me, did not even acknowledge that I was there. She simply sat in her bed and stared, all day long. It was . . . very hard on my father."

Longarm nodded. "I'm sure it must have been. Was this before or after he challenged Tom McCabe's claim the first time?"

"After. He had already lost that land he considered his, and then . . . well, my mother was lost to him, too, even though she was still alive. She lived for almost ten years, but she might as well have been dead. I would not have blamed my father if he had turned away from me, too, in his grief, but he did not. He is a good man, Marshal Long. You must realize that."

"I don't have anything against him," Longarm said honestly. "I'm not on one side or the other in this fight, Señorita Montoya. I just don't want a range war to break out."

"Then let us hope that your judge will see the truth."

Longarm didn't know what to say to that, so he changed the subject by asking, "How well do you know Emily McCabe?"

Mercedes looked a bit surprised by the question. "We grew up on neighboring ranches, so naturally we saw each other from time to time. She's a few years younger than I am. We have never been good friends, if that is what you mean."

"Were you surprised when she married Tom McCabe?"

"I did not know her well enough to be surprised one way or the other. I would have thought she regarded McCabe more as a father than anything else, since her own father died when she was so young. And her mother as well, of course."

"I hear she was pretty much raised by the woman who took over as the cook after Emily's mama passed on."

Mercedes nodded. "Rosaria Canales. A good woman, from what I hear. I did not know her at all."

The way she phrased that caught Longarm's attention. "The Canales woman—is she still alive?"

"I assume so. She returned to her home in Mexico several years ago."

Longarm had halfway assumed that the serving woman he had seen at the Box MCC was Rosaria Canales, but he realized now he had been wrong. He couldn't see that it mattered, but it was another bit of information to file away in his head.

"You must have been shocked when your father proposed marriage to Mrs. McCabe."

Mercedes's eyebrows arched. "Yes, but I want my father to be happy. Whatever it takes to make that so—"

"Some folks might think he proposed because that was one way of getting his hands on the McCabe ranch. If he couldn't win the lawsuit, he could marry his way into control instead."

Mercedes looked coldly at him, and he knew he had angered her. "Don Alejandro Montoya would not do such a dishonorable thing," she stated. "I will not pretend to know all his reasons, but I know his proposal was an honorable one."

"I'm sure you're right," Longarm said, although he wasn't sure of that at all. "Some folks are just too blamed suspicious."

"Yes," said Mercedes. "They are."

They finished their meal, and Longarm said, "I reckon I'd better be going. I surely appreciate your hospitality, señorita."

"It was my pleasure, Marshal Long." Mercedes stood up to walk out with him.

As they went along the hallway from the plaza to the outer door, a painting on the wall caught Longarm's attention. He paused to look at it more closely. The painting was a portrait of a man in the prime of life, a very handsome man with midnight-black hair and a sweeping mustache of the same shade.

"My father as a young man," Mercedes said. "And there is my mother, on the other wall."

Longarm turned and looked, seeing a portrait of a beautiful young woman who bore a striking resemblance to Mercedes. She was dressed in an expensive gown and had a mantilla around her shoulders and a comb in her upswept blonde hair.

"She was lovely," Longarm murmured.

"Yes, she was. Those portraits were done in Spain, not long after they were married. Just before they came here, in fact. My father had gone to Spain for the wedding."

"An arranged marriage?"

"Yes. But they could have been happy together if my mother had not hated this land so."

Longarm looked at the portrait of the young Don Alejandro Montoya again and tried to imagine what it must have been like for the man, married to a woman who had lost her mind and no longer even knew him. That was almost enough to make a fella go crazy himself, Longarm thought. But Montoya had hung on somehow, had found something to live for. His daughter, of course, and this ranch that had been in his family for centuries, but maybe something else, too . . .

Suddenly, something tugged at the back of Longarm's brain, something he had seen or heard without really recognizing all the implications of it. It was there in his head for a second and then gone, vanished like a phantom, a will o' the wisp. And no matter how hard he tried, he couldn't grasp it again.

"Marshal, are you all right?" asked Mercedes. "You are frowning as if something is wrong."

Longarm shook his head. "No, just a stray thought that stampeded on me. I reckon it'll come back another time if it was important." Acting on impulse, he reached out and took Mercedes's hand. He lifted it to his lips and kissed the back of it. "Thank you again for your hospitality, Señorita Montoya."

"You are very welcome, Marshal. Perhaps you will come again sometime?"

Longarm looked into her lovely face and smiled. "I reckon you can count on it," he said.

Chapter 14

Nobody took any potshots at Longarm on his way off the Lariat spread, so he supposed Montoya's men were heeding the orders not to start any trouble. In fact, the ride back to Palmerton was downright peaceful.

To Longarm's surprise, so were the next couple of days. He spent them talking to people in town and on the smaller ranches in the vicinity, trying to find out if anyone had a strong enough grudge against Tom McCabe to have ambushed him. As far as Longarm could determine, while McCabe had not been well-liked in the valley, most folks had respected him and had not been bitter enough toward him to stoop to murder. Of course, some of the people he talked to could have been lying to him, Longarm knew, but he had confidence in his ability to know the truth when he heard it, at least most of the time.

So what it came down to, he decided, was the same triangle he had been aware of from the beginning—the rivalry between McCabe and Montoya, plus the added angle of Sam Kingston's designs on the Box MCC. Somewhere in there was the answer to Tom McCabe's murder.

On Monday evening, Longarm was sitting on the porch of the Valley Hotel with Sheriff Walcott when a buggy came rolling along the street. The driver brought the vehicle to a stop in front of the hotel and called out, "Hello, Orville, you old horse thief!"

With a grin, Walcott stood up and stepped over to the edge of the porch. "Careful with that horse thief talk, Judge," he said. "We got us another lawman here, and he might take you serious-like."

Longarm came to his feet as the newcomer climbed down from the buggy and tied his team to the hitch rack. He stepped up onto the porch and shook hands vigorously with the sheriff, who then turned to Longarm and said, "Marshal, this is Judge Michael Davis. Judge, meet Deputy Marshal Custis Long."

"Long, eh?" Judge Davis said as he shook hands with the rangy lawman. "I've heard of you. Surprised we've never crossed paths before."

"Just never had that good fortune, I reckon," said Longarm.

The judge was a tall, slender, middle-aged man wearing spectacles over keenly intelligent eyes. His black suit and flat-crowned black hat were dusty from the trail. He took off the hat, revealing thinning gray hair, and knocked some of the dust off it. "Everything quiet here in town, Orville?" he asked.

"For the time bein'," replied Walcott. "Ain't no guarantee it'll stay that way, though."

"There are no guarantees in life," said Davis, "except that it's a struggle we all must wage."

"That's the damned truth."

Davis turned to Longarm. "I got a wire from Chief Marshal Vail informing me that he'd assigned you to this case, Marshal Long. How does the situation look? Are we still on the verge of a range war?"

"It could come to that," Longarm admitted. "A lot depends on how the court case goes."

"But I'll have to decide in favor of one side or the other," Davis pointed out, "and when I do the other litigant will be unhappy with the decision."

"Yep, that's right."

"So I'd best be prepared to duck as soon as I've adjourned, just in case bullets start to fly," Davis said dryly.

Walcott took his arm. "Come on down the street, and I'll introduce you to Ross Thayer. He's the lawyer for Miz McCabe."

Davis hung back. "It would be a bit improper to meet with counsel for one side without counsel for the other side being present."

"Yeah, I reckon," said Walcott with a shrug. "I hadn't thought of it like that. Looks like you ain't got much choice in the matter, though, 'cause here comes Thayer now."

The attorney was indeed striding along the boardwalk, Longarm saw. Thayer hesitated when he noticed the three men standing on the hotel porch, but then he came on. With a nod, he said, "Good evening, Sheriff, Marshal Long."

"Ross, this here is Judge Davis," Walcott said. "He's worried about doin' something improper, so I guess all you two can do is shake hands and say howdy, then you'd better move along."

"Of course." Thayer took Davis's hand for a second. "It's my pleasure, Judge. I look forward to arguing my case in front of you."

"And I look forward to hearing it," Davis said. "I'll see you in court tomorrow, counselor."

Thayer smiled and walked on toward his office, and acting on a hunch, Longarm went with him. The lawyer seemed a little surprised to look over and see Longarm striding along beside him.

"Something I can do for you, Marshal?" he asked.

"Wouldn't mind talking to you for a few minutes," Longarm said. "I've got a few questions about the case, and about Tom McCabe."

"Of course." They had reached one of the emporiums. A set of stairs led up the outside of the building to a door on the second floor. Thayer indicated the stairs and said, "My office is right here. Come on up."

They climbed the stairs and went inside after Thayer unlocked the door. The office was fairly small and made to seem even more so by the shelves full of law books on the walls and the big, paper-cluttered desk in the center of the room. Through a partially open door on the other side of the desk, Longarm saw a cot and a ladder-back chair. That was probably where Thayer slept. The attorney pulled that door closed and then sat down behind the desk, indicating that Longarm should have a seat in front of it in a straight-backed chair.

The place was a little shabby, Longarm thought, indicating that maybe Thayer's law practice wasn't exactly booming despite the fact that he represented one of the largest ranches in the valley. Longarm took out a cheroot and lit it while Thayer was filling a pipe.

Once they both had their smokes going, Thayer asked, "Now, what would you like to know, Marshal?"

"Montoya doesn't really have much of a case against Mrs. McCabe, does he?"

"Not at all," Thayer said confidently. "If Tom hadn't been killed and the case had gone to trial as originally scheduled, Montoya would have lost. Just like he's going to lose now."

"There are no questions about McCabe's original claim to his spread?"

Thayer puffed on his pipe for a second, then said, "You have to understand, Marshal, most of this valley was open range when Tom came here. The land was there for whoever wanted to take it and use it—and whoever could hold it. But as the years went by, things changed. The territory became more civilized. So Tom filed all the proper claims in Santa Fe. I have the papers in my safe. Everything is absolutely legal and aboveboard."

"What about the Montoya grant? That wasn't open range."

"Of course not. The Treaty of Guadalupe Hidalgo stated that those land grants would be honored, providing that the grantees had proper documentation. Alejandro Montoya does not."

"Was he using the land west of the creek when McCabe got here?"

"No, and that's what caused the problem. The land was sitting there, perfectly good graze being unused, and so Tom moved his cattle onto it. Once Montoya got wind of it, he had his vaqueros haze Tom's cattle back toward the ranch headquarters. Tom's men moved them right back. It went back and forth like that for a while, and there was almost some shooting several times. Then they sent for the land commissioner, and when he arrived from Washington and asked to see Montoya's grant, Montoya couldn't produce it." Thayer shrugged. "That was it, right there. Without any evidence to the contrary, the commissioner decided Tom's claim to the land was just as strong as Montoya's. Stronger, once Tom had legally filed on it in the capital."

"You're a mite too young to have seen all this with your own eyes, though," Longarm said.

Thayer chuckled. "Yes, of course. While that was going on, I was still a youngster back in Pennsylvania. But I heard all about it from Tom before he died, after I'd become his lawyer. A man named Buchanan used to handle Tom's legal affairs, but he passed away several years ago. Tom gave me all the paperwork relating to the case, and I reviewed it thoroughly. There's no doubt in my mind that he was in the right, and of course, that holds true for Emily now."

"Sure sounds like it," Longarm said. "I guess we'll find out over the next couple of days, while the trial is going on."

"It shouldn't take that long. It's really an open-and-shut case."

Coffins were open and shut, too, but Longarm refrained from pointing that out.

"Got any idea who shot Tom McCabe?"

The abruptness of the question caused Thayer to raise his eyebrows. "The first answer that springs to mind is Montoya, of course."

"What about other possibilities?"

Thayer toyed with his pipe for a moment, then leaned forward. "Being an attorney, I shouldn't speculate without any proof . . . but I'd look long and hard at Sam Kingston if I were you, Marshal. I don't think that man would stop at murder to get something he wanted, and he wants the Box MCC. He offered to buy it, but Tom laughed in his face and threw him off the ranch. That's another reason Kingston could have wanted him dead."

Longarm blew a smoke ring. "I thought about Kingston, and that fella who works for him, Nash Lundy."

"A cold-blooded killer. You can tell by looking at him."

Longarm shrugged. "Kingston knew that McCabe and Montoya were wrangling over that land. How would killing McCabe help Kingston get his hands on the ranch?"

"He could have hoped that once Tom was dead, he could buy the place cheap from whoever inherited it. I suppose he thought that was going to be Warren. No one except Tom and I knew that he intended to leave the ranch to Emily."

Longarm's eyes narrowed. "Emily didn't know she was going to inherit it?"

Thayer spread his hands and said, "I can't really speak to that question. Certainly, Tom could have told her. I have no way of knowing. But I didn't tell her, and as far as I know she never saw the will until it was read after Tom's death."

That was interesting, Longarm thought, even though it didn't really prove anything. He had already pretty much ruled out Emily as a suspect in her husband's death, but if he could be sure she was unaware of the provisions of McCabe's will, that would really put her in the clear.

Thayer went on. "As far as the trouble between Tom and Montoya goes, remember that not all of the Box MCC is in dispute, only the sections along the creek. Even if Montoya were to win the lawsuit—which he won't—the rest of the McCabe ranch would be a good prize for Kingston. Combined with the Diamond K, that would make for the largest ranch in the valley."

"But if Mrs. McCabe wins—and if she was to marry Kingston—" Thayer's hand clenched on the pipe. "Ridiculous!" he said. "Kingston only proposed marriage after Montoya did. It's absurd to think that a . . . a lovely young woman like Emily would marry either of them!"

"Pretty far-fetched, all right," Longarm agreed. "Well, I've enjoyed our talk, Thayer. I reckon all that's left to do now is wait and see how the trial plays out."

"We'll win. I've no doubt of that, Marshal."

Longarm just shrugged, unwilling to commit either way. He was just here to see that things followed the law and didn't turn deadly.

Or any more deadly than they had already been, he thought.

Chapter 15

The trial was held at the county courthouse, and it was warm in the courtroom despite the large windows that were open on both sides of the room. Longarm was standing in the back of the courtroom, arms crossed, as Sheriff Walcott, serving as the bailiff, called out, "All rise! Federal district court for the Territory o' New Mexico is now in session, the Honorable Judge Michael Davis presidin'."

Everyone stood as Judge Davis came out of the small room behind the bench. He sat down, rapped his gavel sharply, and said, "Be seated." When everyone had resumed their seats, Davis went on. "The first matter before this court is the lawsuit brought by Alejandro Montoya, a resident of this territory, against Mrs. Emily McCabe, also a resident of this territory. Are the parties to this suit in court?"

A short, pudgy man wearing spectacles stood up at one of the tables in the front of the room. He had a round face and brown hair parted in the middle and slicked down. He pushed his spectacles up on his nose and said, "The plaintiff is present, Your Honor. I am Garrett Berglund, attorney at law, representing Señor Montoya."

So Montoya had himself an American lawyer, Longarm thought. Probably not a bad idea.

At the other table, Ross Thayer rose to his feet. "The defendant is also present, Your Honor, and is also represented by counsel. I am Ross Thayer, attorney at law."

Longarm thought that if folks settled their differences by having their lawyers fight it out, Thayer would probably win easily. Berglund didn't look like much of a scrapper. Of course, appearances could be deceiving.

Longarm let his gaze wander around the courtroom. Montoya sat beside Berglund at one table, while Emily was next to Thayer at the other. Behind the tables where the plaintiff and the defendant and their lawyers sat, a railing with a gate in it divided the room. Several rows of chairs were behind the railing, and most of them were full. Interest in this case ran high in Palmerton and the surrounding area, as well it should. The outcome might well have an effect on the whole valley.

Mercedes Montoya was in attendance, sitting in the first row behind the plaintiff's table. She was dressed in a dark brown jacket and skirt, with white lace showing at the cuffs and collar from the silk blouse under the jacket. Longarm thought she looked lovely.

So did Emily McCabe, who wore a dark blue dress and had her long black hair pulled back and tied at the nape of her neck. She looked around and met Longarm's gaze for a second, but he couldn't read anything in her eyes. She was sure keeping herself on a tight rein, he thought.

None of the punchers from either the Box MCC or Lariat were in the courtroom, though Longarm had seen some of them in town earlier this morning. Longarm was glad they weren't attending the trial. They would have had to relinquish any weapons at the door—as lawmen, he and Walcott were the only men in the room who were armed—but even unarmed, a bunch of proddy cowboys and vaqueros could start a hell of a ruckus.

Emiliano Rafferty was among the spectators. So was Sam Kingston, who had pomaded his unruly hair and put on a suit but still managed to look rumpled and unkempt. Longarm didn't see any sign of Nash Lundy.

From the bench, Judge Davis said, "I'll hear opening arguments. Mr. Berglund?"

The stocky lawyer got to his feet. In his high-pitched, reedy voice, he said, "Your Honor, this matter is one of simple justice. A significant portion of the ranch now known as the Box MCC, owned by the defendant, Mrs. McCabe, is legally the property of my client, Don Alejando Montoya, granted to his family by the King of Spain over two hundred years ago and held in legitimate succession until it was unlawfully seized by Thomas McCabe, the defendant's late husband. Don Alejandro has petitioned the defendant to return to him what is legally his, but since she refuses to do so, he has no choice except to regretfully bring suit against her to regain his rightful property. Thank you, Your Honor."

Judge Davis had listened to the speech impassively. Now he turned to the defendant's table and said, "Mr. Thayer?"

"Thank you, Your Honor," Thayer said as he stood up. "This is a matter which never should have come before the court, because it was legally decided years ago." He picked up a document from the table and brandished it dramatically. "I have here a decision dated September 27, 1854, and written by United States Assistant Land Commissioner Daniel Cunningham—"

"Objection!" Berglund was on his feet. "These are opening statements, and counsel is attempting to introduce evidence!"

Thayer said, "I am merely identifying this document, Your Honor, not introducing it as evidence." He shot a glance at Berglund. "Yet."

"I'll allow you to continue, Mr. Thayer, but please remember that these are opening statements, as Mr. Berglund correctly points out."

"Thank you, Your Honor. As I was saying, this decision written by Land Commissioner Cunningham states that in the absence of the original document granting property to the Montoya family from the King of Spain, there is no evidence to substantiate Señor Montoya's claim. Based on that, I would ask that no more of the court's time be wasted on this matter, and I move for an immediate dismissal of the lawsuit."

"Objection!" Berglund was on his feet again. "He can't do that until it's his turn!"

"Sustained," Davis said without hesitation. "When the plaintiff has rested his case, Mr. Thayer, you may then move for a dismissal if you still wish to do so. But *I* will decide what is and is not a waste of this court's time."

"Of course, Your Honor," Thayer murmured.

"Anything else?"

Thayer shook his head. "We're ready to proceed if they are."

"We're ready," Berglund stated.

Davis leaned back in his chair. "Then call your first witness, Mr. Berglund."

Longarm lifted a hand to his mouth to cover a yawn. He had seen scores of court proceedings, and with only a few exceptions, they had bored the hell out of him. Something about listening to lawyers talk just naturally made him sleepy. With his back braced against the rear wall of the courtroom, he stood up a little straighter. He had to stay alert in case of trouble.

Garrett Berglund said, "I call Don Alejandro Montoya, Your Honor."

Montoya stood up stiffly and moved to the witness chair. Sheriff Walcott came over to him carrying a battered old Bible and swore him in. After Montoya had stated his name for the record, which was being scribbled down at a side table by a pasty-faced gent who reminded Longarm of Henry back in Denver, Berglund asked, "How long has your family lived in this valley, Don Alejandro?"

"Over two hundred years," Montoya said proudly.

"How did they come to be here?"

"In gratitude for service to the king, one of my ancestors was granted title to the lands extending from the mountains in the east, across the creek, and on to the west, to the place known as Arroyo Rojo."

Thayer said, "Objection. The facts of this so-called land grant are not in evidence."

Berglund gave him a withering glance. "I am merely attempting to establish the parameters of my client's claim, Your Honor."

"Go ahead, counselor," Davis said. "I'll overrule the objection."

Berglund smiled, but Thayer didn't seem bothered, Longarm noticed. The victory won by Berglund was a mighty small one.

Turning back to Montoya, Berglund asked, "How far west of the creek is Arroyo Rojo?"

"The arroyo does not run perfectly straight, and of course

neither does the creek. But it is about three miles, I would say."

"And the area bounded by the creek on the east and Arroyo Rojo on the west runs how far north and south?"

"Approximately ten miles."

"So the area in question represents approximately three hundred square miles?"

Montoya nodded solemnly. "This is correct."

"This area was part of the original land grant from the King of Spain to your ancestor?"

"Si."

"Would you repeat your answer in English?"

Montoya looked a little annoyed, but he said, "Yes. The area was part of the original land grant."

"You know this for a fact?"

"I do."

"How?"

"The land is Montoya land. It has always been Montoya land." The don's voice shook slightly with emotion. "My family has fought for it, bled for it, died for it. It will always *be* Montoya land."

Longarm looked at Thayer and saw that the lawyer was smiling. Montoya's testimony might be dramatic, but it didn't have any legal weight without evidence to back it up.

Berglund said, "I have no further questions at this time, Your Honor," and went back to the table.

Davis looked at Thayer, who was already getting to his feet.

"Señor Montoya," Thayer said as he approached the witness, "do you have the actual land grant document signed by the King of Spain?"

"It has been over two hundred years," Montoya said. "Parchment grows old. Things can happen, documents can be misplaced—"

"Do you have the land grant document, Señor Montoya?" Thayer asked again, more heavily this time.

Montoya stared angrily at him for a long moment before saying, "I do not. It is lost."

Berglund popped up. "Just because we are unable to produce the document at this time, Your Honor, does not mean that it does not exist."

A bit impatiently, Judge Davis said, "Your own client says the document's lost, counselor. That seems like a pretty simple statement to me."

Berglund subsided. "Yes, Your Honor, of course."

Thayer asked Montoya, "Have you challenged the right of Thomas McCabe to claim the land in question before bringing this lawsuit?"

"You know I have," snapped Montoya.

"In 1852?"

"Yes."

"And the result of that challenge was that an official of the United States government ruled that you had no legal claim to the land?"

"He was wrong!" Montoya shouted. The old man lifted a clenched fist and shook it. "What do you expect? He was a damned gringo—"

"Your Honor!" Berglund practically yelped. "My client is understandably upset after having been badgered by Mr. Thayer. I humbly ask that you excuse his emotional outburst."

The courtroom was buzzing now. Judge Davis rapped several times with his gavel to quiet the place down, then said, "Please keep yourself under control, Señor Montoya. If you don't, I'll have to find you in contempt of court, and that won't help your case."

Montoya still looked like he wanted to take a swing at Thayer, but he managed to nod and say, "*Si*, Your Honor. I will remember."

Davis said to Thayer, "Go ahead, counselor."

"Thank you, Your Honor." Thayer turned back to Montoya. "Did the United States land commissioner rule against your claim?"

"He did," Montoya said tightly.

"And has the situation changed since then? Have you found the original land grant, for instance, or is it still missing?"

With an effort, Montoya grated, "The situation has not changed."

"So you still have absolutely no evidence to support your claim?"

Montoya sat there silently, his face like stone.

"I won't ask the court to force you to answer that question, Señor Montoya," Thayer said. "Would you say that you brought suit against the late Thomas McCabe, the original defendant in this case, and then against his widow, Mrs. Emily McCabe, in an effort to annoy, embarrass, or otherwise harass them?"

"No!" Montoya's rein slipped and he surged to his feet. "I want what is mine! McCabe was a thief!"

For the first time, Emily spoke up. "That's not true!" she exclaimed as she leapt to her feet.

Davis was already pounding again with his gavel. "Mrs. McCabe, sit down!" he shouted over the tumult in the courtroom. "Señor Montoya, sit down *now*! Order, blast it!"

Longarm wasn't leaning casually against the wall now. He stood up straight, his hand ready to reach for his gun if need be. On the other side of the room, Sheriff Walcott was just as tense.

The judge kept rapping his gavel on the bench, and slowly the noise in the courtroom died down. Thayer went to Emily's side and eased her back into her chair, speaking quietly in her ear as he did so. Berglund hurried up to the witness chair and put a hand on Montoya's shoulder. Montoya shook off the attorney's hand, and for a second Longarm thought he was going to clout Berglund one. Then, reluctantly, Montoya sat down, and Berglund retreated to the plaintiff's table.

"Do you have any more questions for this witness, Mr. Thayer?" Judge Davis asked.

"Just a couple, Your Honor," Thayer said as he left Emily sitting at the table. "Señor Montoya, when Land Commissioner Cunningham ruled that without the original document your land grant was no longer valid, you actually had no legal claim to *any* of your ranch, did you?"

Montoya blinked at him. "What do you mean?"

"Under the circumstances, Tom McCabe could have gone to the territorial capital in Santa Fe and not only filed legal claim to the land that is now known as the Box MCC ranch, he could have also claimed all of your land. Isn't that true?"

"That . . . that is true, I suppose." For the first time, Montoya's proud veneer was beginning to show some cracks. "But the land in dispute was only the area between the creek and Arroyo Rojo."

"Yes, but if Tom McCabe was the greedy, land-hungry thief you make him out to be, he could have taken your entire ranch and forced you out of the valley completely. And you wouldn't have been able to do a thing about it without the land grant document."

Montoya glowered up at him, but he didn't deny what Thayer had said.

"So, actually, Tom McCabe was being a good neighbor. He just took what he thought was rightfully his, and he left you alone to file legal claims on what is now known as the Lariat ranch. Which you have done, correct?"

"I try to abide by the American laws," Montoya said. "My claims are registered in Santa Fe."

"Yes, they are. I have copies of them." Thayer nodded and said to the judge, "No further questions, Your Honor."

Berglund was sitting at the plaintiff's table looking stunned. "Mr. Berglund?" Davis prodded him. "Call your next witness."

Slowly, Berglund climbed to his feet. "I, ah, have no more witnesses, Your Honor. Before Señor Montoya steps down, however, I would like to ask him one more question."

Davis looked at Thayer, who waved a hand confidently, indicating that he had no objection.

Berglund approached the witness. "Señor Montoya, before the land grant document was lost, did you ever see it personally, with your own eyes?"

"I did," Montoya said. "I saw it many times as a young man."

"And is it your testimony, based on your personal knowledge of the land grant, that the document set forth the boundaries as you indicated earlier?"

"I told the truth," Montoya said. "The western boundary was Arroyo Rojo, not the creek."

"That's all, Your Honor," Berglund said.

Thayer stood up. "Can I follow up on that, Your Honor?"

"Go ahead," said Davis.

"Señor Montoya, is there anyone else who actually saw the document and can testify that you are correct about what it said? Anyone at all?"

"The document was old," Montoya said hesitantly. "It was kept locked in a safe. Only members of the family were ever allowed to see it. It was precious, like an heirloom."

Thayer indicated Mercedes with a sweep of his hand. "Should I call your daughter to the stand and ask her if she has ever seen the document?"

"There is no need to do that," Montoya said. "The land grant disappeared when Mercedes was only a child. If she ever saw it, she would have no memory of it."

"So there is no one alive who can corroborate your testimony based on personal knowledge?"

Montoya sighed. "No."

"Thank you." Thayer went back to his chair.

Davis looked at Berglund, who shook his head glumly. "The witness may step down," Davis told Montoya, who stood up and went back to the plaintiff's table, moving like an old man now. Longarm glanced over at Emily and saw that she was watching Montoya with something like pity in her eyes.

Berglund got up and said, "The plaintiff rests, Your Honor."

Thayer was on his feet before Berglund had sunk disconsolately back into his chair. "Your Honor, due to the fact that the plaintiff has introduced no evidence to substantiate his claims, and in light of the decision rendered previously by a United States land commissioner, I move that this lawsuit be dismissed."

Davis grunted. "Now's the right time, counselor." He lifted his gavel, poised to strike. "The defense's motion is granted. This lawsuit is hereby dismissed due to lack of evidence." The gavel came down with a sharp crack. "Next case!"

Longarm waited tensely for the explosion that might come.

Chapter 16

He didn't have long to wait. Montoya leapt up from his chair, shouting, "This is an outrage! Again the gringo government steals from me what is mine!"

Furious, Judge Davis pointed his gavel at Montoya. "One more word and I'll have you arrested, sir!"

Longarm caught some movement from the corner of his eye. The courtroom door was open a couple of inches, and through that gap Longarm caught a glimpse of Chuy Valdez's face. Valdez disappeared. Longarm knew the young vaquero was probably on his way to let Montoya's men know that their *patron* had lost in court.

Sheriff Walcott moved toward Montoya to be ready in case the judge ordered him to take the old man into custody. Meanwhile, Mercedes stepped through the gate in the railing and hurried to her father's side. She took hold of his arm and began speaking quickly to him in an effort to calm him down. Montoya looked as if he wanted to pull away from her, but he didn't try to.

Thayer hugged Emily in congratulations, holding her a little longer than was absolutely necessary, Longarm thought. Most of the spectators were on their feet now, so Longarm pushed his way through them until he reached the railing. Not bothering with the gate, he swung his long legs over the barrier and stepped up to Emily and Thayer.

"Might be a good idea to head on back out to the ranch,"

Longarm said. "Hell could start popping around here in a few minutes."

"But we won," Thayer said, confused by Longarm's warning.

"Don Alejandro doesn't have to accept the loss gracefully," Emily said. "I know I wouldn't, if it were the other way around."

No, she probably wouldn't, Longarm decided, and he thought again how much Emily and Montoya were alike, despite the hostility between them.

"Valdez was skulking around out in the hall and went to spread the word," Longarm said. "That's why I think it would be a good idea if you two got out of here. I'll go with you."

"My buggy's tied up right outside the courthouse," said Thayer. "We'll go straight to the ranch, Emily."

She nodded. "All right. I suppose that would be best."

As they started to turn toward the door, Montoya abruptly pulled away from his daughter and leveled a finger at Emily. "I withdraw my proposal of marriage!" he flared. "I thought to make peace between our families by joining them, but now there can be no peace!"

Sam Kingston bulled forward, holding his hat in his hand. "She was never gonna marry you anyway, you old rapscallion! Hell, you shoulda been ashamed o' yourself for askin'. Miss Emily, *I'm* the one you oughta marry. I can take care o' you and protect you from the likes o' this greaser."

A spate of Spanish curses burst from Montoya's mouth. Sheriff Walcott moved to get between Montoya and Kingston. Over his shoulder, he snapped, "Shut up, Kingston. You're just makin' things worse."

Judge Davis started pounding his gavel on the bench again. "I didn't adjourn the court! Damn it, is anybody listening to me?"

Not much, Longarm thought as he tried to steer Emily and Thayer toward the door, away from both Montoya and Sam Kingston. Kingston called after them, "Just say yes, gal, and we'll have ourselves the biggest spread in the whole danged territory!"

Longarm, Emily, and Thayer had almost reached the door. It burst open in front of them, and half a dozen of Montoya's vaqueros shoved into the room, Chuy Valdez among them. All of them wore guns, leading Judge Davis to yell, "Sheriff, disarm those men! No weapons in the courtroom!"

Disarming those angry vaqueros was going to be even harder than it sounded, Longarm thought. But he and Walcott had to try.

Before they could do so, someone out in the corridor shouted, "There they are! Get 'em!"

Longarm recognized the young, impulsive voice of Jackson Flynn, the Box MCC hand who had traded shots with Valdez on the evening Longarm had first come to Palmerton. Longarm waited grimly for the sound of shots to come from the hall, but instead the doorway and the corridor beyond it turned into a wild melee of flailing, kicking, and punching. Fists thudded against flesh as the McCabe riders led by young Flynn waded into the Montoya vaqueros. Men grunted and cursed loudly. The chaos threatened to spread into the courtroom, which was already a mass of confusion because of the crowd of spectators.

Walcott appeared from somewhere at Longarm's elbow. "Take 'em out the window!" he said. "Get movin' before this turns into a real riot!"

It was just about there already, Longarm thought, but he started pushing a path toward the nearest window anyway, holding Emily's arm and tugging her along behind him. Thayer had hold of her other arm, and together they made sure she didn't fall and get trampled as the fracas spread like wildfire. Judge Davis was still working his gavel and shouting, but no one paid any attention to him now.

Longarm reached the window and threw a leg over the sill. The courtroom was on the first floor, so he was able to step down to the ground without much trouble. He turned back and reached up to help Emily as she climbed out of the building. Thayer scrambled out after her, looking none too pleased at having to make such an undignified escape.

Longarm looked around and saw no one close by, although the noise of fighting from inside the courtroom was growing louder. He took Emily's arm again and asked Thayer, "Where's that buggy?"

"This way," Thayer said, hurrying toward one of the side streets.

They reached the lawyer's buggy a moment later. Thayer helped Emily into the vehicle and climbed in after her. Longarm stepped back and took off his hat as Thayer picked up the reins. "Make for the ranch! I'll follow along after," Longarm said, then he slapped the horse on the rump with his Stetson. The horse took off running, with Thayer struggling to keep the buggy under control.

Longarm didn't like to leave Sheriff Walcott alone to cope with the brawl inside the courtroom, but he didn't want to leave Emily unguarded for any longer than necessary. Now that the lawsuit was over and she had won, she might turn out to be in even greater danger than before. If anything happened to her, the Box MCC would be left in the hands of Warren McCabe. Warren wouldn't be any match for either Montoya or Kingston, and with them crowding in from both sides, they could carve up the McCabe ranch between them.

This was a hell of a mess, Longarm thought as he headed for the hotel corral to saddle his rented mount. If he had been able to find out who had bushwhacked Tom McCabe, it might have simplified matters. If he could have laid his hands on that old land grant document and proven one way or the other what it said, that would have helped, too. But at the moment, both of those things seemed pretty far out of reach.

He threw his saddle on the steeldust in a hurry, swung up onto the horse, and galloped out of Palmerton, taking the main trail north. He didn't see any other riders, and he was thankful for that. Since he could move faster on horseback than Thayer's buggy could travel, within a quarter of an hour he spotted the vehicle rolling along the trail in front of him.

He caught up to the buggy quickly and waved for Thayer to keep going. A glance over his shoulder showed Longarm no dust rising from the trail, so maybe they hadn't been followed. But anybody who knew this part of the country could probably come after them without necessarily having to stay on the trail. They might even find trouble waiting for them when they got back to the Box MCC.

Thayer had the buggy moving so fast that the ride was pretty rough on Emily, but it was better for her to get bounced around a little than to be caught out here in the open by folks who wanted her dead. Longarm kept a close eye on both sides of the trail, watching for any sign of an ambush, but nothing happened during the hour it took to reach the McCabe ranch house.

Ed Jordan came running from the barn as Thayer brought the buggy to a sliding stop in front of the house, raising a cloud of dust in the process. "What's wrong?" Jordan yelled. "You came down the road like you had a pack of Apaches on your tail!"

"The trial's over," Longarm said as he swung down from the steeldust and pressed the horse's reins into Jordan's hand. "Mrs. McCabe won, but Montoya's declared war on her."

"Damn it! I was afraid it'd come to this."

"It'll be all right, Ed," Emily said to her foreman as Thayer helped her from the buggy. "I'm sure Don Alejandro will calm down once he understands there's nothing he can do to change things."

Longarm wasn't going to count on that. "Take Mrs. McCabe in the house," he said to Thayer. "I'll be there in a minute."

The attorney hustled Emily into the ranch house. Longarm was glad the place had such thick log walls. They would stand up to a lot of rifle fire if it came down to a siege.

"Some of your hands were in town, fighting with Montoya's men," Longarm told Jordan. "I saw that young fella Flynn. Looked like he was one of the ringleaders."

"Jackson's a hothead, all right," said Jordan, "but he's a good kid. Mighty loyal to Miz McCabe. Was there any shootin'?"

Longarm shook his head. "Not by the time we lit a shuck out of there, just a heap of fisticuffs."

"Maybe nobody got killed, then," the foreman said worriedly.

"How many men do you have here on the ranch?"

"Half a dozen or so. The rest are either in town or out on the range."

Longarm nodded. "Better than nothing. Get 'em armed and set some of them out as guards. We'll need some warning if Montoya attacks the place."

"Right. You fortin' up in the house with Miz McCabe and that lawyer?"

"Yeah. We could use you and another man inside with rifles to help us cover as many windows as possible."

"Be there in a few minutes, as soon as I get those lookouts posted."

Longarm nodded again, satisfied that Jordan could do an adequate job of setting up the ranch's defenses. He clapped a hand on the middle-aged cowboy's shoulder in gratitude, then hurried inside.

He found Emily and Thayer in the parlor. Emily was sitting in an armchair with her hands knotted together in her lap, while Thayer paced back and forth worriedly over a Navajo rug. "I should have foreseen that Montoya wouldn't abide by the court's ruling," Thayer said when Longarm came into the room. "I suppose I placed too much faith in the power of the judicial system. All I knew was that we had an open-and-shut case."

There he went with that open-and-shut business again, thought Longarm. He said, "It looked like Montoya's daughter was trying to cool him off. Maybe she'll get lucky and keep him from coming after Mrs. McCabe."

"What about Sheriff Walcott?" Emily asked. "Can't he stop Don Alejandro?"

"Walcott's just one man with a couple of deputies," Longarm said. "Montoya's got a hundred men or more in his crew. If he's determined to come out here and settle things by force, it might take the army to stop him."

Thayer said, "Well, then, why don't we call on the army for help? We could wire the nearest fort—"

Longarm shook his head. "That'd take too long. I reckon we'll have to hold out by our lonesome, if it comes down to that."

"Damn that man's pride!" Emily burst out. "He and Tom were just alike, stubborn as mules." Her chin came up defiantly. "He's going to find out that I can be just as stubborn as he is."

Longarm went to a gun rack on the wall and took down a Winchester. There was a set of drawers under the rack, and when he opened the top one he found several boxes of ammunition, as he had thought he would. He started feeding .44 cartridges through the rifle's loading gate.

"Problem with stubbornness," he commented, "is that it sometimes gets folks killed."

Emily's face paled. "Yes, that's true, I suppose," she murmured. "I was so angry I hadn't thought about that. But what can I do? I can't marry him, and I'm not going to just give him half my ranch."

"You can marry me," Thayer said abruptly. "You know I—"

"Ross, please don't," Emily cut in. "Not now. This isn't the time or the place."

Determinedly, Thayer said, "When will be the right time, Emily? I've tried to respect Tom's memory—"

Again he was interrupted, this time by Ed Jordan. The foreman hurried into the parlor and said to Longarm, "I got those guards set out, Marshal, and got a couple of fellas in the barn with rifles and shotguns. Nobody's goin' to sneak up on us, which ain't the way Montoya would do it anyway."

"No, he'll come at us from the front, guns blazing, if he comes at all," Longarm agreed. He levered a shell into the chamber of the Winchester and then tucked the rifle under his left arm. "And I reckon we'll be waiting."

Chapter 17

The afternoon passed slowly, and as Longarm stood at one of the windows and looked out at the trail leading up the valley from Palmerton, he wished he knew what had happened back in town. The fracas in the courthouse was surely over by now. He hoped no one had been seriously injured.

Emily had grown more worried as the day went on, too. She had brushed off Thayer a couple more times when he tried to bring up his feelings for her, and the lawyer had retreated to an armchair in front of the massive, unlit fireplace, where he was still sulking.

While Longarm was standing by the window, Emily came over to join him. In a quiet voice, she said, "I've been thinking, Marshal . . . do I bear some of the blame for all this?"

"For the trouble with Montoya, you mean?" Longarm shook his head. "I don't rightly see how. There was bad blood between Montoya and your husband before you were even born."

"I could have given him the land when he wanted it."

"I reckon you thought if you did that, your husband would be rolling over in his grave."

Emily smiled sadly. "He certainly would have. Tom never liked Don Alejandro. He respected him, but never liked him."

Longarm kept one eye on the trail outside as he said, "Seemed to me that for a second there in the courtroom, you felt sort of sorry for Montoya."

"I suppose I do," Emily said. "He's lost so much over the years. His wife was insane, you know."

"So I've heard."

"I remember when she came over here one time."

Longarm's eyes narrowed. "Montoya's wife came here to the ranch?"

"That's right. I was very small, probably no more than three or four, but for some reason I remember that night very well. Probably because she frightened me so badly."

"What happened?" Longarm asked, curious.

"Well, Don Alejandro had to keep her locked up most of the time. He was afraid she would hurt herself, I think. But she got out somehow one evening and managed to get on a horse. I have no idea what she was trying to do or where she was trying to go, but she found her way over here somehow. She rode in screaming . . ." Emily's face flushed warmly. "Screaming about a whore. I didn't know what she was talking about at the time, of course, but I'll never forget the way she looked. She wore an old dress that was dirty and had gotten torn on the brush, and her hair was wild, so matted and tangled that I don't see how anyone could have ever combed it out. She was a very beautiful woman when Don Alejandro married her and brought her here, I've heard, but by that time—"

"I've seen her portrait," Longarm said quietly. "Spitting image of her daughter Mercedes."

"Yes, I suppose so."

"What happened after she rode over here?"

"Tom went out and tried to talk to her. He told me about it years later. He wanted to calm her down so that he could get her back over to her home. But she fought him and grabbed his gun out of its holster, and I think she might have hurt herself or someone else if Rosaria hadn't managed to talk to her."

"Rosaria? The lady who helped raise you?"

Emily nodded. "My mother and father had been dead for a couple of years by then. Rosaria had such a gentle way about her that she was able to convince Señora Montoya to give her the gun. She took her into her room and kept her there while Tom sent a rider galloping over to Lariat. Don Alejandro and some of his men came to get her and took her home in a wagon." Emily sighed. "That was the only time I ever saw her. She died not long after that. There was a rumor that she might have . . . taken her own life, but I don't know about that."

"Montoya's had it sort of rough, all right," agreed Longarm. "But that don't excuse murder."

Emily looked intently at him. "Do you think he had something to do with Tom's death?"

"I don't know about that," Longarm replied honestly. "But if he tries to kill you, that'll be attempted murder, plain and simple." Not wanting the conversation to get too grim, he changed the subject by asking, "Whatever happened to Rosaria?"

Emily smiled. "A few years ago she went back to the village in Mexico where she was raised. She still has family there, and since she was getting older, she wanted to be with them again."

"You ever hear from her?"

"I get a letter every now and then. Rosaria can't read or write, herself, but she gets one of her grandchildren to write what she wants to say. They were educated at the mission school in her village."

"I reckon you must miss her some."

"Yes," Emily said softly, "I do. She was like a mother to me."

Longarm had heard the same thing about Rosaria Canales. He found himself halfway wishing the woman was here now, so that she could help Emily bear up under the strain, because Emily was definitely feeling it. After a moment, she clenched her hands together again. "God, I wish all this had never happened. Maybe Tom should have left the ranch to Warren."

"Where is your brother-in-law?"

"Up in his room. He has no idea what's going on, I'm afraid. He asked me if I brought any licorice back from town for him." Her voice broke a little. "I had to tell him that I didn't have a chance to go to the store. He said it was all right, but he asked if I'd get him some next time."

Montoya wasn't the only one who'd had a rough life, Longarm thought as he looked at Emily McCabe. From being orphaned at such an early age to having the husband she loved bushwhacked and killed, she'd had a lot to endure. She was holding up so far, but Longarm sensed that her strength was growing more fragile.

She confirmed that by saying, "I feel rather weak right now, Marshal. Would it be all right if I went up to my room and lay down for a while?"

"Of course," Longarm said. "This is your house. You can do whatever you want. Might ought to stay away from the windows up there, though, just in case."

Emily nodded. "All right." She hesitated, then added, "Thank you for everything you've done. I can see now I never should have let the situation get to this point. You're putting yourself in danger for me. So are Ed and the other men."

"Jordan and the rest of the boys ride for the brand," said Longarm. "And as for me, well, Uncle Sam pays me for what I do. Not as well as he should, mind you, but I ain't complaining."

Emily smiled at him and went to the stairs. As she started up them, Thayer got to his feet and looked like he was about to follow her. Longarm caught the lawyer's eye and shook his head. "Mrs. McCabe wants to lie down for a while," Longarm told Thayer. "Reckon we'd best give her some peace and quiet."

For a second, Thayer looked like he was going to argue, then he shrugged his shoulders and said, "Fine. If trouble comes she'll probably be better off upstairs anyway."

Longarm went back to devoting his full attention to the trail from Palmerton. He smoked a cheroot as he looked out the window, and he smelled Thayer's pipe tobacco and knew that the lawyer was smoking worriedly as well. Thayer was still brooding and not talking, so the room was quiet.

As Longarm watched and waited, his mind inevitably strayed. He found himself remembering the odd feeling that had come over him when he looked at the portrait of a young Don Alejandro Montoya. Impossible as it seemed, there was something familiar about that portrait, Longarm realized, as if he had seen it before. But he had never been to this valley, had never met Montoya, and had never been to the Lariat ranch until the visit when he'd had lunch with Mercedes and looked at the paintings of Montoya and his wife.

The sun slid down toward the western horizon, and try as he might, Longarm couldn't figure out what it was that kept nagging at his brain. His stomach wasn't happy, either. He hadn't eaten since breakfast. This job was causing him to miss too blasted many meals. He thought longingly about the food at Emiliano Rafferty's cantina, and that made him think about Lita, and that gave him a hunger of a completely different sort. Rafferty probably had pegged him as being on the side of Emily McCabe in the dispute, and while that wasn't really true—Longarm would have stood up for Montoya just as quickly if the evidence had backed the old man—he had a feeling he wouldn't be having any more pleasant meals at the cantina. And if Rafferty found out about what Longarm and Lita had been doing, that would probably come to an end, too.

Longarm's mind was drifting, but his eyes were as keen as ever. He spotted a haze of dust floating in the air between the ranch and the lower end of the valley, where the town was located, and as he watched, the dust grew into a cloud of the stuff, boiling up from the trail. A lot of riders were coming, and they were coming in a hurry.

"Company coming!" he called out, loudly enough for Ed Jordan and the other man on guard in the house to hear him. Carrying the Winchester, he went to the door and stepped outside to look toward the barn. One of the men there had spotted the dust cloud, too, and was waving toward it. Longarm nodded and retreated back into the house. Everyone was alerted, so all they could do now was wait.

The group of horsemen came in sight, following the trail as it curved alongside the creek. Thayer joined Longarm at the window and said anxiously, "What do we do now?"

"You have a gun, counselor?"

Thayer reached under his coat. "A small pistol."

"Are you any good with it?"

"Not really. I'm a decent shot with a rifle, but I haven't had much practice with a handgun."

Longarm jerked a thumb toward the gun rack. "Get one of those Winchesters and load it, then. But keep that pistol handy, too. The little ones aren't much good except for close work, but it could come to that."

The riders had started out as mere dark dots at the base of

the dust, but by now they were individual figures. Longarm estimated there were at least fifty of them. As they came closer, he could tell that many of them were wearing high-crowned, broad-brimmed sombreros. Vaqueros, he thought. Montoya's men.

So it really was war.

Longarm opened the window and bellowed across at the men in the barn, "Hold your fire unless they start the ball!" A hand emerged from the door of the hayloft and waved acknowledgment of the command.

The riders swept up to the ranch house and reined in. Longarm spotted Montoya sitting on a big black horse in the lead. The old man didn't look as spry as he had been on his previous visit. His face seemed gray and drawn. But maybe that was just because of the dust, Longarm told himself.

Montoya's horse took a couple of mincing steps forward. "Señora McCabe!" Montoya called. "We must talk!"

Longarm hoped Emily had the sense to stay upstairs. Since Montoya hadn't come in shooting, there might be a way to talk this through without anybody getting killed, but Longarm was afraid Emily's stubbornness and temper might get the better of her if she confronted Montoya herself.

From one side of the open window, Longarm called, "This is Marshal Long! You can talk to me, Don Alejandro!"

Montoya glared toward the window. "Where is Señora McCabe?"

"Don't worry about that," Longarm told him. "Her lawyer is here with me, and we'll handle any talking. What do you want?"

"I came to tell her that a dozen of her men are in jail in Palmerton. Sheriff Walcott arrested them on charges of disturbing the peace."

Longarm bit back a curse. Once the brawl was over, Walcott really wouldn't have had any choice except to throw Flynn and those other reckless young punchers in the hoosegow, he supposed, but it would have been nice to have the odds a mite more even. Longarm asked, "What about your vaqueros? They were fighting, too."

"I have paid their fine and had them released," Montoya replied.

"Damn it," Longarm muttered. He hadn't been thinking

far enough ahead. Now the Box MCC would be short-handed in any fight, even after the riders who were out on the range came back in. And the Lariat crew had been larger to start with, too.

"You've brought the message," Longarm called through the window. "We'll take care of it. Much obliged."

"Señora McCabe and I have other business to discuss."

"I don't think so," Longarm said. "You heard the judge's decision. You don't have a legal right to any of her land."

"The judge was wrong!" For the first time during this encounter, some of Montoya's previous fiery nature came back to him. "That land will always be mine! It was paid for with Montoya blood!"

"So you figure on killing Mrs. McCabe and taking it?" Longarm knew he was running a risk by throwing a challenge in Montoya's face that way, but he was tired of beating around the bush.

Montoya looked shocked. "I do not make war on women," he declared. "If Tom McCabe was still alive, there would be powdersmoke in the air by now as well as this accursed dust." Montoya shook his head. "But I cannot harm this young woman, no matter how stubborn she may be."

"My God," whispered Thayer, "he sounds like he means it."

"He does," Longarm told the lawyer in an aside. "He was bred to be an honorable man."

Montoya walked his horse closer. "Marshal Long, may I speak to Señora McCabe? I am a proud man, and there are things I must say to her alone."

Longarm hesitated. As unlikely as it had seemed a few hours ago, he had the feeling that Montoya wanted to make peace. If that was the case, then this was an opportunity they couldn't pass up.

He inclined his head toward the stairs and said to Thayer, "Go get her."

"What? Have you lost your mind, Marshal?" Thayer was pretty agitated, and Longarm wished he hadn't told the lawyer to arm himself with a rifle. "This is a trick," Thayer went on. "It has to be."

"I don't think so," Longarm said. "You go get Emily, and I'll let Montoya in."

"I don't like it—"

"You don't have to like it," Longarm snapped, finally losing patience. "Just do it."

Thayer glowered at him, but after a second he started toward the steps. Longarm turned back to the window and called, "You can come into the house and speak with her, Don Alejandro. You and you alone."

Montoya drew himself up in the saddle. "You think to make a hostage of me?"

"Nope. Just being careful."

Montoya considered the proposition, then abruptly nodded. "Very well." With the awkwardness of advancing age, he climbed down from the saddle. Instantly, one of his men spurred forward to take the reins of his horse. It was Chuy Valdez, Longarm saw. Valdez looked fit to bust, he was so anxious for hell to pop, but he wouldn't go against the orders of his *patron*.

Longarm went to the front door and unbarred it as Montoya stepped up onto the porch. Holding the rifle in his right hand, Longarm used his left to swing the door open. Montoya stepped over the threshold. The gaze he turned toward Longarm was coldly contemptuous, but he managed to give the lawman a civil nod and muttered, *"Gracias."*

"De nada," Longarm told him. "I sure hope you and Mrs. McCabe can work things out, Don Alejandro. Seems to me like the valley ought to be big enough for—"

The clatter of frantic footsteps on the stairs made Longarm stop short and turn in that direction. He saw Ross Thayer coming down from the second floor, a look of wide-eyed shock on his face. "What the hell?" Longarm said. "Where's Mrs. McCabe?"

"She's gone!" Thayer blurted out as he reached the bottom of the stairs. He said it again, clearly unable to believe the words that were coming from his own mouth. "Emily's gone!"

Chapter 18

"You lie!" Montoya exclaimed. "Where could she go?"

"I swear she's gone." Thayer was practically babbling by now. "I went to her room and knocked on the door, and when she didn't answer I thought she must be asleep. I opened the door and . . . and—"

"Come on," Longarm said grimly. "Let's go have a look."

He led the way up the stairs with Montoya and Thayer close behind him. Not knowing which room was Emily's, he had to step aside to let the lawyer go in front of him down the second-floor hallway. Thayer flung open the door to one of the rooms and said, "See? She's not here."

Longarm stepped into the doorway and looked around the room. The covers on the bed were rumpled, as if someone had been lying on them earlier, but no one was there now. The room was empty, just as Thayer had said.

"This is a trick," Montoya said angrily. "You seek to hide her."

"I was just as surprised as you were," Thayer said. He seemed to be regaining some of his composure now that the other two men saw that he wasn't lying. "Emily came up here to rest earlier this afternoon, and that's the last we've seen of her, isn't it, Marshal?"

"That's right," Longarm said. "I give you my word on that, Don Alejandro."

"But if this is true . . . where could she have gone?"

"We'd better have a look around the rest of the house," Longarm decided.

The three men were turning away from Emily's door when the next door along the hallway opened. Warren McCabe looked out at them as they stopped. "Hello," he said. "Is it suppertime yet?"

"Warren!" exclaimed Thayer. He started toward Warren, and the older man stepped back, surprised and evidently frightened by the lawyer's intensity.

"I'm sorry," Warren said. "I didn't mean to upset you, Ross."

Thayer grabbed hold of Warren's arms. "Have you seen Emily?"

"Em-Emily?" Warren repeated, confused and still scared. "Not for a while."

"How long ago, Mr. McCabe?" asked Longarm, hoping that a calmer tone would calm down Warren as well.

"Mr. McCabe." Warren mustered up a laugh. "Nobody ever calls me that. Tom was Mr. McCabe. I'm just Warren."

"When did you see Emily, Warren?" Longarm asked gently. He put a hand on Thayer's shoulder and squeezed, and Thayer let go of Warren's arms.

"Let me think . . . it was a while ago, I know . . . I asked her if she had any licorice for me—"

"After that," Longarm said, knowing that Emily had had that conversation with Warren soon after they returned to the ranch.

Warren began to nod. "Yes, I saw her. I remember now. She came back upstairs after that. She knocked on my door. I asked her if I could go riding with her. She said I couldn't, not this time."

"How do you know she was going riding?"

"Well, she had on those clothes she wears when she goes riding. You know, those trousers like a man's trousers, and that old hat."

Longarm asked, "What else did she say after she told you that you couldn't come with her?"

Warren scratched his head and frowned in thought. "I remember she hugged me . . . I always like it when Emily hugs me, she's so nice and soft and she always smells really good—" Warren's face lit up as he recalled something else.

"Oh, she said good-bye, that was it. She hugged me and said good-bye and told me she would see me when she got back."

"Where was she going?" Thayer grated before Longarm could ask the question.

Warren frowned. "Now, that's what I didn't understand. No, sir, I didn't understand it at all. She said she was tired of all the trouble and that she was going home. Yes, sir, going home. But this is her home, isn't it? Hasn't she always lived here?"

"She has no other home," Montoya said. "The girl was born on this ranch."

"He has to be telling the truth," snapped Thayer. "Warren's too dumb to lie."

Longarm saw the hurt expression that appeared in Warren's eyes, and he thought about how good it would feel to plant a fist in the middle of Thayer's face. That wouldn't solve the bigger problem, though, which was Emily McCabe's disappearance.

"If Mrs. McCabe sneaked out and rode off right after she came up here, that means she's got a couple of hours head start," Longarm said. "And night's coming on. I'd better get after her."

"My men and I will come with you," said Montoya.

Longarm looked over at the old man and shook his head. "I don't reckon that'd be a good idea."

Montoya drew himself up rigidly. "I told you, I want peace. I am too old for war."

"Maybe you are, but some of your vaqueros might not be. I mean no offense, Don Alejandro, but I want you and your men to go on back to Lariat and stay there. I'll find Mrs. McCabe and bring her back, and when I do, then maybe the two of you can sit down and talk it all out." Longarm didn't think they would be able to reach any sort of agreement unless one of them gave in—which wasn't likely to happen—but he didn't say that.

"You would go after her alone?"

"I'm used to tracking folks," said Longarm. "That's a big part of my job." He glanced at Thayer. "Unless you want to come along, counselor."

Thayer looked torn. "I'm not much good on a horse," he finally said. "And I'm no good at tracking at all."

Longarm nodded. "That's all right." He hadn't much wanted Thayer's company to start with. "Maybe one of the hands saw her leaving and can point me in the right direction."

"What if they didn't?" Thayer asked. "How will you know where to look for her?"

Longarm scraped a thumbnail along the line of his jaw. "I've been thinking about that," he said, "and I've got an idea of another place that Emily just might consider home."

There were back stairs in the house; that was how Emily had gotten down from her room without Longarm and Thayer seeing her, Longarm quickly discovered when he took a look around the place. From the kitchen it would have been simple for Emily to dash across to the barn without calling attention to herself.

The chestnut mare she had been riding when Longarm met her on the ridge where Tom McCabe had been bushwhacked was gone. The mare had been in the corral behind the barn, but neither of the men who had been posted there had heard anything unusual. Longarm figured all their attention had been focused on the threat that might be coming up the valley toward the ranch, and so they hadn't noticed when Emily slipped into the corral, saddled the mare, and led the horse out. She probably hadn't mounted up until she was well away from the house.

But then, if she was determined to get away from all the trouble that was plaguing the valley, she would have put the mare into a ground-eating gallop. She could be miles away by now, Longarm knew.

He found tracks that he thought belonged to the mare leading west away from the ranch headquarters. It was difficult to tell how old the hoofprints were, but his instincts told him they were the ones he needed to follow. He headed the steeldust west, too. His saddlebags were stuffed with enough supplies to last him almost a week, and he had a box of .44 cartridges that was almost full. There was plenty of water in this part of the country, but that might not be true elsewhere, so he also took along a couple of canteens.

As he rode toward the western mountains, he worried about what might happen in the valley while he was gone.

Sheriff Walcott would do his best to keep the peace, Longarm knew, but if the local lawman had been confident in his ability to keep the lid on, he never would have wired Billy Vail for help in the first place. Montoya had given Longarm his word that he would keep his vaqueros under control, so Longarm wasn't too concerned about trouble coming from that direction.

Sam Kingston was still sitting over there on the Diamond K, however, just waiting for the chance to make a grab for the McCabe ranch, and with Emily missing, he might think this was a prime opportunity. Not only that, but Longarm knew word would get around quickly about Emily being gone. If anything were to happen to her—if she wound up dead and never came back to the Box MCC—then Warren would inherit the ranch. Talk about a lamb lying down with lions, thought Longarm.

And Nash Lundy was a cold-blooded killer. He wouldn't think twice about gunning down a woman. If he somehow got to Emily first . . .

This was a race, Longarm realized, and the stakes were Emily McCabe's life. He had the advantage over Lundy right now, but that lead might not hold up. Longarm had to see to it that it did.

After he had followed the tracks west for a few miles, the trail began to swing to the south. That fit in with the hunch Longarm had about where Emily might be going. She had tried to throw off any pursuit by heading west at first, but now she was headed toward her true destination. Before long, Longarm was riding due south, toward the Mexican border.

He pushed the steeldust as hard as he dared. With the suddenness common to Western twilights, night closed down around him. Longarm rode on a short distance, then reined in and started looking around for a place to camp. Even though stopping chafed at him, he didn't want to risk losing Emily's trail in the darkness. She would probably stop for the night, too, so at least she wouldn't be gaining on him. He hoped.

He unsaddled the steeldust and let it graze on a hillside under some trees. At the bottom of the hill was a tiny creek, little more than a trickle. Longarm made his camp there. He saw a faint glow on the horizon some miles to the east and figured it came from the lights of Palmerton. Out here, though, darkness lay all around him.

Since he didn't want to advertise his location, he made a cold camp and gnawed on a biscuit and some ham he had brought from the McCabe ranch. It was possible Sam Kingston had heard about Emily's disappearance by now, and he could have sent Lundy out on her trail. The last thing Longarm wanted to do was to lead the gunman right to her.

Using his saddle for a pillow, he stretched out and fought the urge to smoke a cheroot. Nearby, the horse cropped contentedly on the grass. Longarm looked up at the stars sprawled across the black velvet sky above him and wondered why folks had to fight over land when it seemed to him like there was plenty of room for everybody. The frontier was a hell of a big place, after all.

He knew he wasn't going to be able to puzzle it out. Human nature was just too blasted complex for there to be any simple answers. So he rolled over and went to sleep instead.

Chapter 19

Longarm was mounted and on the trail at sunup the next morning. By the time a couple of hours had passed, he had reached the southern end of the valley and ridden past it into a more arid landscape dotted with scrubby mesquite and cactus. The openness of the terrain made it easier for him to keep an eye on his back trail, but on the other hand it made him easier to follow from a distance, too.

It was a little before noon when he noticed the rider behind him.

Longarm kept moving, not wanting the pursuer to realize that he had been spotted. The rider wasn't taking any great pains not to be noticed; in fact, he was pushing his horse hard enough so that a tendril of dust climbed into the air to mark his location. Longarm eased up on the pace, willing to sacrifice a little of the ground he hoped he had gained on Emily in order to deal with whoever was back there behind him. He started watching for a good spot to lay a trap.

A half-hour later he came to a gully that slashed across the ground from west to east. The banks on both sides were gentle enough so that he could have crossed it easily, but instead after riding down into the cut, he turned to the right. The gully twisted and turned every few yards, so he rode around the nearest bend and then reined the steeldust to a halt. Swinging down from the saddle, he tied the horse's reins to the roots of a bush that protruded from the side of the arroyo. He slid the Winchester from its saddle sheath and waited.

He was rewarded by the sound of rapid hoofbeats a short time later. Whoever was chasing him was coming on quickly. Longarm stood silently at the bend until he heard the sliding of rocks and dirt that meant the rider was coming down the bank into the gully. Then he stepped around the corner, brought the Winchester to his shoulder, and yelled, "Hold it right there, old son!"

He expected to see Nash Lundy, expected as well that the gunman would try to throw down on him. Longarm was ready to fire, his finger tense on the trigger. He saw the horse, a big black, come sliding to a halt at the bottom of the bank, and the rider turned a startled face toward him.

Mercedes Montoya.

Longarm had just enough time to recognize her before her horse, startled by his shout, reared up on its hind legs and pawed the air. Mercedes was just as startled as the horse was, and with a panicked cry she fell from the saddle. Longarm heard the hard thump as she landed on the ground.

At least neither of her feet had tangled in the stirrups, he thought as he lowered the rifle and sprang forward. The black was dancing around skittishly, and he was afraid the horse would stomp on Mercedes if he didn't get it away from her. He grabbed the dangling reins and tugged the horse down the arroyo.

When he had some distance between Mercedes and the horse, he dropped the reins and hoped the black would stay ground-hitched. He swung back around toward Mercedes and stopped abruptly as he saw that she was sitting up and pointing a pistol at him.

"Better be a mite careful with that, ma'am," he said, trying to keep his voice cool and calm. "They tend to go off."

The revolver was a Colt .45 Peacemaker, a good-sized gun for a woman to handle, but the barrel didn't waver as she kept it lined on him. "Don't worry, Marshal, I know how to use a gun. It won't go off—unless I want it to."

Longarm believed her. He said, "No need for shooting. I'm sorry I spooked your horse. I figured you were somebody else."

"Who?" Mercedes demanded.

"Nash Lundy."

She grimaced. "That *cabron*. Do you think to insult me?"

Longarm couldn't help but grin. "No, ma'am. Once I got a look at you, I knew you weren't Lundy. You're a whole heap prettier."

That was certainly true. Mercedes wore a black vest over a white shirt, and her black riding skirt had hiked up when she fell so that her calves and knees were exposed over the boots she wore. Her hat had fallen off, and her blonde hair fell freely around her shoulders.

The compliment made the Peacemaker's barrel droop a little. "I'm lucky I didn't break a leg when I fell off Apache, you know."

"Apache would be that horse of yours?"

"That's right."

"Nice-looking animal, but he spooks pretty easy."

"He's not accustomed to having a man point a rifle at him and shout at him. Neither am I."

Longarm grunted. "Said I was sorry. Don't know what else I can do, so if you're planning on shooting me, you might as well go ahead."

Now Mercedes lowered the Colt all the way to her lap. "You can come over here and help me up," she suggested.

Longarm walked across the sandy floor of the arroyo and extended a hand. Mercedes reached up to take it, and he hauled her to her feet. She slipped the Colt back into the black leather holster on her hip and then used both hands to dust off the bottom of her skirt. She winced as she did so, and Longarm knew her rear end would be sore and bruised after she'd landed on it so hard.

"Sorry," he said.

"My own fault, I suppose. I should have known that I couldn't just ride up behind a man such as yourself. You're too watchful, and too ready for violence."

"Handy habits to have in my line of work," Longarm pointed out.

"I am sure they are."

"Just what is it you're doing here?" he asked her. "You're a long way from home."

"I was trying to catch up to you, of course."

"Why in blazes would you want to do that?"

"You're looking for Emily McCabe, aren't you?"

Longarm nodded. "That's right. I suppose your father told you she's run off?"

"Yes," Mercedes said with a nod of her own. "I came to help you find her."

"What makes you think you can do that?"

"She is going to see Rosaria Canales, is she not?"

Longarm was a little surprised Mercedes had come to the same conclusion as he had about Emily's destination. The only place other than the Box MCC he could think of that Emily might consider home was the Mexican village where she could find the woman she regarded as her second mother. But how had Mercedes known that?

When he asked as much, she shrugged. "As I told you, Emily and I have known each other since we were girls. We were never close friends, of course, but I know how she felt about Rosaria."

"Maybe you were closer than you realized," said Longarm. "After all, both of you were raised pretty much without your real mama."

"This is true," murmured Mercedes. "I can understand how Emily must feel, being in the middle of all this trouble that is not of her own making. She needed someone to turn to, someone who could comfort her. Who better than Rosaria?"

"All right," Longarm said. "We've hashed that out. Now we have to figure out what to do with you, so I can get back on the trail."

Mercedes said, "You take me with you, of course. That was my intention from the start." She moved her hand to her rear end again for a second. "I had not counted on being so rudely welcomed, though."

Longarm tried not to grin. He said, "You can't go with me. You'd better head on back to Lariat."

Mercedes gave a stubborn shake of her head. "I can help you," she insisted. "I know how to find the village where Rosaria Canales now lives."

Now that was interesting, thought Longarm. "How do you know that?" he asked.

"I have relatives in Mexico, remember? I have traveled to see them many times. Rosaria's village is not far from one of the main roads. I can show you."

"I could just follow Emily's trail," Longarm pointed out.

"I can take you there more quickly."

"What if that's not where she's going?"

"Where else could it be?"

Longarm didn't have an answer for that. He knew logically that Mercedes was right. He also knew that he didn't want to be saddled with taking care of her while he was trying to retrieve Emily. He wasn't going to be satisfied that they were out of danger until they were back on the McCabe ranch, and even then things still wouldn't be settled.

Mercedes tossed her head, sending the blonde hair swirling around her shoulders. "You can send me back," she said, "but I won't go. I'll still come along behind you."

"You're pretty good at being a nuisance, aren't you?"

She laughed. "Of course. I have had much practice. I am rich and my father's only child."

"Why are you so danged anxious to help me find Mrs. McCabe?"

Mercedes grew solemn again. "I want peace in our valley, Marshal. That can never be until she and my father have come to an agreement. Otherwise there will continue to be trouble, and sooner or later someone will be killed."

"Tom McCabe's already dead," he reminded her.

Anger flared in her eyes. "My father had nothing to do with that, and neither did any of our men."

"You're sure about that?"

"I would swear it on my poor mother's grave."

Longarm tended to believe her. He was leaning toward the same conclusion himself.

He rubbed a thumbnail along his jaw. "Did you tell anybody at Lariat where you were going, or did you just sneak off like Emily did?"

"I told no one. My father would have forbidden me to come, and if I had told any of the vaqueros, they would have gone straight to him. They still think of me as a child to be protected."

Mercedes Montoya was far from a child, Longarm thought. She was a grown woman with a mind of her own and no hesitation about expressing her opinions. And she handled a Colt pretty good, too, he added mentally.

"Somebody's liable to come after you," he said.

"I know. But we can reach the village of Rosaria Canales first and find Emily."

"You reckon you can keep up?"

"Try me," she said defiantly. "In his sleep, Apache could outrun that horse of yours."

"We ain't fixing to have a race," Longarm said dryly, "but I intend to get where we're going as soon as possible."

"Why are we standing here in this arroyo wasting time, then?"

She had a point. Longarm shrugged and said, "Get your horse."

As he turned toward the bend where he had left the steeldust, she said, "There was one more reason I wanted to come with you, Marshal."

Longarm looked back over his shoulder. "What's that?"

"I wanted to spend more time with you. I find you a very interesting man. And quite handsome, in a rugged sort of way." With a smile, she moved on toward her horse.

Longarm frowned. If what he had seen flickering in her eyes like tiny flames was any indication of what he had to look forward to, Mercedes coming with him could complicate things a mite. He just could be looking at more problems.

On the other hand, he'd never been the sort to run away from trouble, either . . .

Chapter 20

With Mercedes now leading the way, Longarm could devote more attention to watching their back trail. They rode on through the day, eating a cold lunch, and it was late afternoon before Longarm saw any sign that someone might be following them. When he looked over his shoulder, he spotted a dust haze far in the distance to the north and reined in.

Mercedes followed suit. "What is it?" she asked.

Longarm turned the steeldust so he was facing north and sat there for a long moment studying the landscape. "Riders back there," he said. "Quite a few of 'em, looks like."

"Some of my father's vaqueros, perhaps. They could be looking for me."

"Maybe." Or it could be Kingston, Lundy, and some of those hardcases from the Diamond K, he mused. He had thought that Kingston might send Lundy alone after Emily, but maybe Kingston had decided not to risk everything on one man. Longarm glanced at Mercedes and asked, "Are we below the border yet?"

She nodded. "Yes, I think so."

"Then I'm out of my jurisdiction."

Mercedes laughed. "I am thinking you are not a man who worries overly much about such things."

Longarm shrugged and said, "I try to do things legal-like . . . when I can. I reckon in this part of Mexico, though, there's not much law to start with except the *rurales*."

"Which means there is not much law," Mercedes said contemptuously. "There is probably not a troop of *rurales* within a hundred miles."

Longarm figured she was probably right. Whatever happened, it would be up to him to keep Mercedes—and Emily, if they found her—safe.

He wheeled the steeldust and said, "Let's go."

They both picked up the pace. The two horses had reserves of strength, and Longarm and Mercedes put them to use over the next hour, pushing the animals as hard as they dared. By sundown, Longarm thought they had gained a little on their pursuers.

"Should we keep moving?" Mercedes asked as darkness began to fall.

Longarm considered the question. "Whoever's back there will probably stop for the night, so I reckon we can, too. The moon's new, so there's not really enough light to follow tracks without taking a risk of losing them." He reached a decision. "If we can find a good place to hole up for the night, that's what we'll do. How much farther do you think it is to the village where Rosaria lives?"

"If we start early in the morning, we will reach it by midday."

Longarm nodded. "Good enough. Watch for a place to camp."

The terrain had gradually grown rougher during the afternoon. The ground was still mostly flat and semi-arid, but mesas thrust up occasionally toward the sky. In the fading light, Longarm spotted one that had a deep cut in its side and some trees clustered around its base. He waved Mercedes toward it.

When they got there, they found that a spring bubbled to the top of the ground and formed a small pool at the spot where the mesa had split, probably sometime eons in the past. The cut was about twenty feet wide and forty feet deep, tapering to a dead end as it ran into the mesa. The floor was sandy and sloped upward slightly. Longarm didn't think they would find a better place to camp. Any attackers could only come at them from the front, and the scrubby trees that grew around the pool offered a little protection from that direction as well. There was enough grass around the pool to give the horses some graze.

"We'll spread our bedrolls inside the cut," Longarm said after they had dismounted and the horses were drinking from the pool. Longarm had already checked the water before letting the steeldust and the black anywhere near it. There was no tang of alkali in the pool. The water was clear and cool and good.

"In its own stark fashion, this is a beautiful place," Mercedes observed.

Longarm agreed. "A good place to fort up, too, if need be."

She laughed. "You men. Must you always be so practical?"

Somebody had to, thought Longarm, but he was smart enough not to say it. Instead, he suggested, "I'll tend to the horses. I think we can risk a little fire back in the cut. It'd sure be good to have some hot coffee again."

"I will do that," Mercedes volunteered. "I know you think of me only a spoiled, pampered child, but I am an excellent cook."

Longarm didn't think of her as a child at all, but he didn't say that, either. Instead, he unsaddled the horses and rubbed them down, then left them to graze undisturbed near the pool. They weren't going to wander far from that water, and they would make excellent sentries in case anybody came skulking around in the night.

Mercedes gathered wood and built a small fire. Not much smoke came from it, and Longarm had to give her credit for knowing what she was doing. She put coffee on to boil and sliced some bacon into his frying pan. The aromas that came from both soon had Longarm's mouth watering.

Together with some of the biscuits from Longarm's saddlebags, the bacon made a fine meal. Nothing fancy, of course, but washed down with strong black coffee, Longarm thought it was delicious. The only thing that would have made it better was a dollop of Maryland rye in the coffee, but unfortunately he didn't have that.

When they were finished he used sand to scrub out their plates and utensils while Mercedes put out the fire. Longarm put everything away, then sat down and leaned back against a small boulder with a sigh of satisfaction. Plenty of trouble still hung over their heads, but for right now, with a full belly and a decent place to sleep, he was content.

Mercedes said, "I was thinking I might bathe in that pool."

The pool didn't hardly seem big enough for that to Longarm, but he wasn't going to tell her that she couldn't try. "Go ahead," he said. "I reckon you want me to be a gentleman and not look."

"I want you to do whatever pleases you," she said as she stood up and began tugging her shirt out of the riding skirt.

Clearly, she didn't mind him watching as she undressed. She took off the black vest and draped it carefully over a rock, then unbuttoned the shirt and placed it over the vest. Her fair skin seemed to glow, reflecting even the faintest starlight. Her bared breasts were small and firm, pear-shaped with nipples that were probably dark brown but looked almost black in contrast to the creamy surrounding flesh.

She put her hands on her skirt and pushed it down over her hips and thighs, then stepped out of it, leaving her clad in silk drawers and high-topped black boots. Extricating herself from the drawers was a little trickier, but she managed to do it gracefully and then stood before Longarm nude except for the boots. The triangle of hair that covered her groin was so fair that it was little more than a barely seen shadow.

"Well, Marshal, what do you think?" she asked with a smile.

Watching her strip like that had caused Longarm's manhood to harden into a throbbing stiffness. His voice was a little husky as he said, "I think you're a beautiful woman, Señorita Montoya."

"I will bathe now," she said.

Longarm's eyes never left her as she walked over to the pool and paused beside it long enough to take off the boots. Then she waded out into the pool and knelt so that she could cup the water and splash handfuls of it over her nude body.

With a little growl deep in his throat, Longarm came to his feet and reached for the buckle of his gun belt.

She turned her head and watched over her shoulder as he undressed. When he was as naked as she was, he padded toward the pool on bare feet. The sand, shaded as it was for most of the day inside the cut, was cool underneath his feet.

Mercedes stood up and turned slowly toward him as he waded into the pool. Her eyes dropped to his manhood, jutting out long and thick and proud from the thicket of dark hair on his groin. "You are as magnificent as I knew you would be," she murmured. "A stallion of a man."

"And you're as pretty a lady as I've run across in a long time," Longarm told her. "But are you sure this is what you want?"

She laughed softly. "Do not worry, Marshal. I am not a blushing virgin. I have had lovers before, when my father and I visited in Mexico City."

"Does Don Alejandro know about that?"

"If he does, he chooses to ignore it." She reached out and boldly closed her fingers around his shaft. "We should not be talking now. The time for that is past."

Longarm couldn't help but agree with her. He took her in his arms and kissed her, his mouth finding her lips open and hungrily waiting for him. Their tongues met and dueled sensuously as she continued caressing his shaft.

Longarm had one hand in the middle of her back. The other slid down to the curve of her hips and explored the soft mounds of her buttocks. She flinched a little, and he remembered how she had fallen off her horse earlier in the day. He took his lips away from hers and muttered, "Sorry."

"Do not be sorry," she whispered. "Just make love to me."

They stood there in the pool toying with each other for long moments. Her skin was slick and cool where she had splashed water over her body. Longarm lowered his head to her breasts and sucked one of the dark nipples into his mouth while he cupped and molded the other pear-shaped mound with his hand. Mercedes stroked his hair and made a noise of pleasure deep in her throat as his tongue swirled around the hard bud of flesh.

Eventually they wound up lying on the sand next to the pool. Mercedes still had hold of Longarm's manhood, using her thumb to spread the moisture that she milked from the slit in the swollen head. When he reached between her legs and explored her feminine folds with his fingers, he found that she was as wet as he was. He slipped a couple of fingers inside her, and that caused her to thrust her pelvis against his hand. Her fingers tightened around his shaft.

She was breathing hard by now, and she panted, "I must have you . . . inside me!"

Longarm moved over her as she spread her thighs wide to welcome him. She brought the head of his organ to her opening and rubbed it up and down along the lips of her sex, lubricating both of them.

"You are so big," she sighed. "I want all of it . . . now!"

Longarm thrust, penetrating her with ease. She was very tight, the muscular walls of her chamber gripping him with surprising strength, and he doubted that she'd had quite as much experience as she had let on earlier. She wasn't a virgin, though, and she clearly knew what to do once the great goad of Longarm's shaft was buried to the hilt between her legs.

The rhythm into which they launched was timeless, universal, and maddeningly exquisite. Longarm began kissing her again. Her breasts flattened against his chest as he allowed some of his weight to press down on her. She moaned against his mouth, and her hands caught at his hips as if to urge him deeper into her. That wasn't really possible, however. Longarm was bottoming out on each downward stroke.

After only a few minutes, Mercedes began to spasm underneath him as her climax swept over her. Longarm felt himself pulled along with her by the power of her culmination. He froze with his shaft buried as deeply within her as it would go and began to empty himself into her. That just made even more powerful shudders go through Mercedes.

Finally, after what seemed like forever, Longarm's climax faded away, and with a long, satisfied sigh, he rolled off Mercedes. They lay side by side on the sand. Longarm propped himself up on an elbow so that he could watch the rise and fall of her breasts as she tried to catch her breath. When she could speak at last, she said, "You certainly . . . lived up . . . to my expectations, Marshal."

He chuckled. "Under the circumstances, I reckon you ought to call me Custis, Señorita Montoya."

"Only if you call me Mercedes."

He leaned over and nuzzled the nipple that was closest to him. "That's fine with me, Mercedes," he said.

"Ah, Custis," she said as she stroked his hair again, "if only you could stay in the valley when your job is done."

Longarm looked up at her. "When I first rode in, I thought that it might be a nice place to retire someday."

"Really?" Her voice had the sound of hope in it.

Longarm didn't want her thinking things that would probably never come true. "The only thing wrong with that," he said, "is that I likely won't ever get to retire. Most gents in my line of work don't."

She let out a little cry. "Do not say such things!"

He shrugged. "Just trying to be honest with you, Mercedes. What we had here tonight was mighty nice, but the chances of it happening very many more times . . . well, they're just not that good."

She sat up sharply. "You are a terrible man! I was so happy, and now I am not. You do not care about me at all."

"I think enough of you that I won't lie to you," said Longarm. "Like you said earlier today, you're rich and your father is a powerful man. Most folks probably tell you just what they think you want to hear. I can't do that."

"You know I am accustomed to getting what I want."

"Sure. But that's not always the way it's going to be."

She pouted for a minute or two, then suddenly reached over and grasped his shaft, which instantly began to harden. "To hell with the future," she said. "We have tonight, do we not?"

Longarm put his arms around her, picked her up, and pulled her onto his lap. He was hard enough again so that he was able to penetrate her as she straddled his hips.

"We damn sure do," he said as her hips began to pump. "We have tonight . . ."

Chapter 21

The night passed quietly, and Longarm and Mercedes were up early the next morning despite not having gotten much sleep because they were too busy enjoying each other's bodies in every way they could think of. Mercedes prepared a quick breakfast while Longarm saddled the horses in the predawn gloom. By the time the sun poked its brilliant orange circle over the eastern horizon, they were both mounted up and riding south.

As they rode, they talked. Longarm said, "I don't mean to bring up painful memories for you, but I'm curious about something. Emily McCabe told me that one time when she was a little girl, your mother rode over to the McCabe place all upset about something. Do you remember that?"

Since the heat of the day had not grown too strong, Mercedes rode with her hat dangling behind her head by the chin strap. Her blonde hair shined in the sunlight as she nodded and said, "I remember, but I am surprised Emily does. I was quite young myself, and she was even younger."

"She said she recalled that night because your mama scared her so."

Mercedes nodded again. "I can imagine that. My mother was a frightening figure, even to me. She must have been terrifying to someone who did not even know her. I remember tiptoeing past her room so very quietly, so that I would not disturb her. When she was upset, she would scream and scream . . ."

Longarm waited for a moment after her voice had trailed off, then said, "I've been trying to figure out why she would go to the McCabe ranch. It's not like she was friends with anybody over there, was it?"

With a shake of her head, Mercedes said, "No. There was never any friendship between my father and the McCabe brothers, and even less so once he had lost his first land claim against them. And the only person over there my mother even knew was Rosaria Canales."

Longarm looked sharply at her. "The cook? The lady who raised Emily?"

"The one we seek now, yes. Rosaria worked briefly for my father when she first left her village and came to the New Mexico territory. But then, after Emily's mother died and Tom McCabe needed a new cook, she went to work for him."

"How'd your father feel about that?"

Mercedes shrugged. "He may have regarded it as a betrayal of sorts. That would be his way. But it must not have bothered him too much, because he seldom spoke of it afterward."

Deep in thought, Longarm tugged on his right earlobe as he rode along. He had been toying with the idea that maybe there had been something romantic, or at least physical, between Don Alejandro Montoya and Rosaria Canales. After all, at the time Montoya had still been relatively young, with the needs of a vital young man, but married to a woman who had lost her mind and probably wanted nothing to do with him that way. And Rosaria would have been handy. If that had been the case, though, wouldn't it have bothered Montoya more for Rosaria to desert him and go to work for his archenemy? Or maybe Montoya had been able to put her out of his head and turn to one of the other young servant women on the ranch . . .

"Perhaps I should not say this," Mercedes resumed after a momentary pause, "but what I really remember about the time Mama ran away from the ranch is how she and my father argued earlier that day."

Longarm looked at her again. "How can you fight with somebody who's crazy?" he asked, then wished he hadn't put the question quite so bluntly when Mercedes winced a little.

She didn't seem to be offended, though. She said, "My mother was insane, but she had moments of lucidity, times when she was clear-headed again and almost her old self. But even at those times, she still hated my father. I heard them that day, behind the door of her room. They were shouting at each other. My father is only human, after all. There were times when the strain of coping with her was too much and he . . . snapped momentarily."

"Did he beat her?" Longarm asked in a hard voice.

Mercedes shook her head. "He never laid a hand on her. But he would shout back at her when she began to rail at him." She looked off at the horizon. "I hated those times. I wished they would both go away." A long sigh escaped from her. "But then my father would leave my mother's room, locking it behind him. I could hear her beating on the door and scratching at it with her fingernails. He would usually take me riding then, so that I would not have to listen to her madness. By the time we came back, she would have gone back to the way she was before, silent and staring. Only on the day you asked me about, she was gone when we returned to the *hacienda*. She had managed to break the lock on the shutters over the window and climb out. My father was frantic when he discovered she was gone. You see, despite everything, he really loved her, and he was afraid she would come to some harm wandering around by herself. He was organizing a search party when a rider from the McCabe ranch came galloping up. He brought the news that Mama was over there. Papa took a wagon and brought her home."

Longarm heard the bleak, tragic quality in her voice and halfway wished that he hadn't forced Mercedes to revisit that awful day in her mind. But he had learned a little more about what life had been like on the Montoya ranch in the past, and what he had learned didn't make him feel more kindly toward Don Alejandro. Fate had dealt Montoya a bad hand when the beautiful young wife he loved had lost her mind, but he had responded to it by locking her away like some sort of animal. Longarm was no expert on such things, but it seemed to him that there should have been something else Montoya could have done for his wife, something that might have helped her. It was all water under the bridge, of course, he told himself, but the waters of the past were what carved out the canyons of people's lives.

As he had been doing all morning, he checked behind them from time to time, and at midmorning he spotted dust. "Damn," he muttered under his breath.

"What is wrong?" asked Mercedes.

"I thought maybe those hombres behind us had lost the trail," Longarm said. "But they're still back there."

Mercedes squinted up at the sun. "In another hour, we will be at the village where Rosaria Canales lives."

Longarm heeled the steeldust into a trot. "Let's try to whittle that down some," he said.

And let's hope that we find Emily when we get there, he added silently.

The village was a haphazard scattering of perhaps two dozen adobe buildings. The largest, dominating the landscape, was an old mission with a tall, square bell tower. At the other end of the single street was the village well, and several women were gathered around it when Longarm and Mercedes rode in. Yapping dogs capered around the hooves of the steeldust and the black. Longarm resisted the impulse to kick at the annoying mutts. Beyond the village, the ground sloped up to a ridgeline of small hills. The slope was covered with cultivated fields, and men were working in them now, wearing straw sombreros and the loose white shirts and trousers and rope-soled sandals of peasants. The women at the well wore black dresses and had their heads wrapped in equally somber scarves. They looked curiously at Longarm and Mercedes. Strangers wouldn't come often to this place, Longarm figured.

But if Emily was here, then Longarm and Mercedes would be the second and third such strangers in the past couple of days.

They reined in beside the well, and Mercedes spoke in rapid Spanish. Longarm savvied the lingo well enough to know that she was asking about Rosaria Canales.

One of the old women pointed down the street at an adobe hut and told Mercedes that was the home of Rosaria Canales. Mercedes said, "*Muchas gracias,*" and turned her horse to ride that way. Longarm walked the steeldust alongside her.

The door of the hut opened before they got there, and a slender figure in a peasant dress stepped out into the noonday sun. The young woman's long black hair was unbound and hung around her shoulders and down her back. She looked right at home here, Longarm thought, as if she herself might be a native of this Mexican village.

And just like that, he knew. Aided by some guesswork, the pieces of the puzzle fell together inside his head.

As they reined in, Emily McCabe shaded her eyes with a hand, smiled sadly, and shook her head. "I should have known you'd come after me, Marshal," she said. "I'd already seen evidence that you were a stubborn man."

Longarm rested his hands on the saddlehorn. "Just trying to do my job, Mrs. McCabe."

"Your job was to see that a range war didn't break out while we were waiting for the trial to start," Emily said rather sharply. "You did that already. The trial's over."

"But it didn't settle anything," Longarm pointed out.

Emily sighed. "No, I suppose it didn't. That's why I left. I was just too tired to deal with it any longer. If it wasn't for Warren, I think I'd just let Don Alejandro and Sam Kingston fight over the ranch."

Longarm knew that wasn't true, but he didn't say anything as Emily's gaze shifted to Mercedes and she asked, "What are you doing here?"

"Hello, Emily," Mercedes said. "I offered to help Marshal Long find you."

"He had no right to find me." Emily's eyes moved back to Longarm. "You can't drag me back there. I don't want to go yet."

Longarm leaned forward in the saddle, and his voice was harsh as he said, "You think by running off you've put a stop to the trouble in the valley? Not hardly. We're not the only ones on your trail. I figure Kingston and his men are looking for you, too, and they won't want to take you back. They'll leave you here—dead."

Emily drew in a sharp breath. "What? Kingston proposed to me—"

"And he might have married you, too, if you'd said yes, but if you'd gotten in his way you wouldn't have lived long.

Now, here below the border where there's not any law, he can kill you and eliminate you permanently as an obstacle to what he wants."

"The ranch—"

"Damn right," said Longarm. "I know what you said about leaving it to Warren, but you both know why you can't do that. He wouldn't last a week before Nash Lundy found some excuse to gun him down. Then it would be open war between the Diamond K and Lariat over the Box MCC. As long as you and Don Alejandro were sniping at each other, Kingston had to hold off. He knew he couldn't fight the both of you. But with you gone . . ." Longarm shrugged, but his meaning was plain.

"Are you saying that . . . that the rivalry with Don Alejandro was actually what was keeping Kingston at bay?"

"That's the way it looks to me," Longarm said.

"So . . . what do I do now?"

Longarm sensed that Emily was beginning to see the true picture and that she wanted to be reasonable. He smiled and said, "First of all, how about inviting us in out of this hot sun?"

"Of course. There's a little pen in the back where you can put the horses."

Longarm swung down from the saddle and tended to that while Mercedes went inside the hut with Emily. He put the horses in the pen but didn't unsaddle them. It might be necessary to leave this village in a hurry, and he wanted to be ready.

When he stepped into the hut, he found Emily and Mercedes sitting on opposite sides of a rough-hewn table and eyeing each other warily. A heavyset Mexican woman with hair that was still dark despite her age was pouring water from a pitcher into cups. Something that smelled good was simmering in an iron pot on the stove.

The Mexican woman placed the cups in front of Emily and Mercedes, and Emily murmured, "Thank you, Rosaria." Longarm had already guessed that he was looking at Rosaria Canales. He had heard so much about her, but until now he'd had no idea what she looked like. Her strong features were indicative of her *Indio* blood. In late middle age, she was still a handsome woman, but not the type who had ever been beautiful. Still, Longarm liked the strength and dignity he saw in her face.

He took his hat off as she turned to him, and Emily said, "Marshal Long, this is Rosaria Canales."

"I'm mighty pleased to meet you, ma'am," said Longarm. "I've heard a lot about you."

"And Emily has spoken of you, too, Marshal," Rosaria said in good English. "Have a seat and I will bring you water. The stew will be ready soon. There is enough for all."

"Much obliged for your hospitality," Longarm told her as he went over to the table and sat down at it. That put him between Emily and Mercedes.

"I still don't want to go back," Emily said stubbornly. "I don't see what good it will do."

"Don Alejandro wants peace," Longarm said. Mercedes nodded in agreement with him. Longarm went on, "He still thinks part of your ranch rightfully belongs to him, but he's always going to feel that way. I reckon he wants to work something out anyway."

Emily laughed hollowly. "Maybe I should see if he'll propose marriage again, and I could say yes this time. How about that, Mercedes? How would you like it if I was your new mother?"

Mercedes paled, and from the stove where she had gone to stir the pot of stew, Rosaria said sharply, "Do not even joke about such a thing, little one!"

"Why not?" Emily laughed. A note of hysteria crept into the sound. "Why shouldn't Don Alejandro and I get married? Then we'll all be one big happy family!"

"Well," said Longarm, "I reckon the main reason you and Don Alejandro can't get married is because he's really your father, Emily."

Chapter 22

The stew pot, which Rosaria had been taking off the fire on the stove, slipped out of her hands and crashed to the floor. The steaming liquid inside splashed out but missed her legs and feet. *"Dios mio!"* she cried, but from the way she was staring at Longarm, it was clear her exclamation was prompted by what he had just said, not the accident with the stew.

Emily and Mercedes were both looking at Longarm like he had grown horns and a tail. For a moment, neither of them could speak, but then Emily said, "*What* did you say?"

"Don Alejandro is your father, Emily."

"No!" Mercedes cried. "It cannot be!"

Emily shook her head. "That's crazy. It's impossible. My parents were Jeff and Nora Griffith. My father was a wrangler, and my mother was the cook."

"I reckon Nora Griffith was your mother, all right," Longarm said gently, "but the man you believed was your father really wasn't."

Emily jerked to her feet. "Stop saying that!"

Mercedes looked equally upset. "It cannot be true," she insisted. "I am my father's only child."

Longarm looked across the room at Rosaria Canales. "Somebody here knows I'm telling the truth. Aren't I, Rosaria?"

Emily swung around toward the older woman. "He's lying!" she said. "He has to be lying. He . . . he has to be . . ."

Her voice trailed off as she read the truth on Rosaria's mournful face.

"I swore to myself I would never tell you," Rosaria said quietly. "And I suppose I kept that vow. It was this man who told you." She gave Longarm a hard, narrow-eyed stare.

"Sometimes the things that went wrong in the past have to come out," he said, "otherwise the present and the future get even worse." He glanced out the open doorway at the sleepy village. Trouble could be approaching quickly, but he knew he couldn't leave things as they were. Emily would never go with him or cooperate with him until he had all the tangles straightened out.

"Don Alejandro got a raw deal," he went on. Emily and Mercedes had fixed their attention on him now. "He went to Spain and married a woman who didn't want to come back to New Mexico with him. But the marriage had been arranged by their families, so she went through with it. Arranged or not, Don Alejandro fell in love with her. Maybe she loved him, too, I don't reckon we'll ever know that. But she sure hated New Mexico. Hated it bad enough that living there drove her insane."

"She was not that way when she came," Rosaria said. "But she missed her homeland more and more with every day that passed."

Longarm nodded, then turned to look at Mercedes. "You came along, and your father hoped that would make things better. It didn't. You know that."

"I know," Mercedes said in a hushed voice.

"So your father turned to somebody else. I figured at first maybe it was Rosaria here, since she worked for him around that time."

"Never!" Rosaria crossed herself. "I am a good woman. I would not commit adultery, no matter how sorry I felt for Don Alejandro."

Emily sat down again and leaned forward. "What you're saying doesn't make any sense," she insisted. "My mother was on the Box MCC, not Lariat. I doubt if Don Alejandro ever even saw her, let alone—" The words choked off as she couldn't finish the sentence.

Longarm shook his head. "I don't know how they got

together. Maybe they were both out riding one day and ran across each other. However it happened, you were the result, Emily."

"I don't believe it," she whispered. "I just don't believe it."

"If somebody just told me, I might not, either," Longarm said. "But I saw it with my own eyes, more than once. The first time I saw you and Don Alejandro jawing at each other, I thought how alike the two of you are. And then, when I was at Lariat and I looked at that portrait of the don as a young man, I saw the resemblance even more. I felt like I had seen the portrait before, when what I had really seen were Don Alejandro's features in you, Emily."

Mercedes looked across the table at Emily for a long moment, then said in awe, "My God, it *is* true."

"No! My father—"

"Maybe Jeff Griffith never knew," Longarm said. "Maybe he suspected. That's something else we can't ever know. But what we do know is that he kept on loving your mama, Emily. No matter what. He loved her so much that after she died, he was so torn up about it that he wasn't watching close enough the day that horse kicked him. Then, with both of them gone, nobody knew who your real father was."

Emily slumped back in her chair, then turned and glared accusingly at Rosaria, who stood nearby with her hands knotted together. "Except you."

Rosaria shook her head. "No, child. Not then. I never knew until . . . until that night—" She couldn't bring herself to go on.

"Until the night Don Alejandro's wife came over to the Box MCC looking for Nora Griffith," Longarm finished for her. "In her condition, she didn't know that Nora had already been dead for a couple of years."

Mercedes lifted a hand to her mouth. "He told her! When they were arguing, he told her about . . . about Emily's mother."

Longarm shrugged. "I reckon that's the way it must've happened. Your father lost his temper and threw it in her face that he'd had an affair with another woman, and so your mother went looking for her." Longarm looked at Rosaria. "That's what she told you that night, after you'd calmed her down and taken her into your room to wait for Don Alejandro to come get her."

Rosaria nodded. "The clearness of her mind, it did not last long. But long enough so that I learned the truth from her and realized who Emily's father must have been. She and I, we were friends while I worked on the Lariat. She said I was her only friend in this godforsaken land."

Emily's eyes widened in horror as another realization hit her. Now that she was beginning to accept the fact that Montoya was her father, the other implications were starting to sink in. "He . . . he knew," she gasped. "He knew I was his daughter, and he still wanted to . . . to marry me . . . to—"

Rosaria came to her and put a hand on her shoulder. "No!" she said. "Don Alejandro never knew you are his daughter. Your mother never told him. Though in his anger he boasted to his wife of his affair, he told her as well that no child resulted from the union. He does not know to this day."

"How could he not know?" Mercedes said. "How could he not see?"

"Some folks are blind to the things they don't want to see," said Longarm. "But somehow, deep down, Don Alejandro must've sensed there was some sort of connection between you and him, Emily. That's why he always stopped short of a range war, no matter how mad he was at Tom McCabe. That's probably why he wants to work out some sort of peace treaty with you now. He may not know you share the same blood, but he knows he doesn't want it spilled." Longarm smiled. "Of course, I'm just guessing."

"You guess too good, Marshal," Rosaria said heavily.

Emily put her hands over her face for a moment, then took a deep breath and lowered them. "No, Marshal Long's right. The truth had to come out, sooner or later." She looked up. "The question is, what do we do now?"

"Get back to the Box MCC as quick as we can," Longarm said. "Then you and Don Alejandro can hash it all out." He added wryly, "Since you're his daughter, too, you might actually have a claim on some of his land, instead of the other way around."

All three women glared at him. "My father must never know the truth," Mercedes said.

"I don't want anything from him," Emily added. "I just

want him to leave me alone to run my ranch."

Rosaria added, "No good would be done by revealing the truth to Don Alejandro. He is an old man. To find out that he had another child all these years . . . the shock might be too much for him."

Longarm frowned. He didn't much like it, but if the don's daughters put up a united front against him, he wasn't sure he had the right to overrule their decision. After all, Montoya was their father, not his.

"All right . . . for now," he said. "You'd better get your gear together, Emily. We've got some riding to do."

"All right," she agreed. "I guess I can't hide anymore."

She stood up and began to stuff clothing into a saddlebag that she took from a bunk. Longarm went outside and started around the hut toward the pen where he had left the horses. Emily's chestnut mare was back there, too, and he could get the animal saddled while Emily was preparing to leave.

He looked to the north, expecting to see the dust cloud raised by their pursuers, then stopped short and frowned as he realized the sky was clear. He had been planning to cut toward the east for a ways before turning north and making a run for the border. But maybe whoever was back there had lost the trail. It wouldn't hurt to hope.

When Longarm had the chestnut saddled, he led all three mounts around to the front of the hut. Emily, Mercedes, and Rosaria had emerged from the little adobe structure, and Emily hugged Rosaria tightly after putting her gear on her horse. "I don't suppose I can convince you to come back with us," she said.

Rosaria shook her head. "My place is here, child. But you must write to me. I will have my grandson read your letters to me—" A sharply indrawn breath cut off her sentence.

"What is it?" asked Emily. "What's wrong?"

"Nothing," Rosaria said quickly. "I just remembered something. Can you wait a moment before you leave?"

Emily looked at Longarm, who shrugged. "As long as it's quick," he said.

"Wait here," Rosaria said. She turned and hurried into the hut. When she came back a few minutes later, she was carrying a small wooden box about a foot long, four inches wide, and four inches deep. She held it out toward Mercedes and said, "This should be yours. It was given to me by your mother. She had it with her the night she came to the McCabe ranch."

Mercedes hesitated, then took the box from the older woman. "What is it?" she asked.

"An old paper of some sort." Rosaria smiled and shrugged helplessly. "I do not know what it says, because I cannot read. And I have never had one of my grandchildren read it for me."

Longarm, Emily, and Mercedes all looked at each other. Emily said, "You don't think—"

"Why did she give the box to you, Rosaria?" Mercedes asked.

Again Rosaria shrugged. "She said it was very important that your father never see it, and the only way I could get her to calm down was to agree to protect it for her. But she is long dead now, may she rest in the peace she never found in life, and so I give this to you to do with as you will."

"Better open it up," Longarm said tightly.

Mercedes swallowed nervously and worked the catch on the latch that held the box's lid closed. She opened it, revealing a piece of parchment that was rolled up tightly and had a piece of ribbon tied around it. Mercedes handed the box to Emily, then untied the ribbon and unrolled the parchment.

"Oh, my God," Emily said quietly.

Longarm saw the fancy Spanish writing and the royal seal, and he knew he was looking at the long-lost Montoya land grant.

Chapter 23

"The paper, it is important, no?" Rosaria asked innocently.

"It is important," replied Mercedes. "Very important."

Emily crowded closer to her, trying to read the wording on the document, her dark head close to the fair one of her half-sister. "The boundaries," she said. "What does it say about the boundaries?"

Longarm was pretty curious about that, too. The elaborate script was hard to make out, but he thought he saw the words *Arroyo Rojo.*

"My father was right," Mercedes said after a tense moment. With a slender finger, she traced the pertinent passage in the document. "The boundaries of the grant are laid out exactly as he said."

"Then part of the Box MCC really is his," Emily said in a half-whisper. For a moment, her shoulders sagged, as if she were unable to believe this revelation. Then she straightened and took a deep breath. "All right. I know Tom honestly believed that land was his, otherwise he never would have fought so hard for it. But if he had seen this document—" She gestured toward the land grant. "He would have given it up right away. He was a law-abiding man. He would want me to follow the law, too. Mercedes, that land belongs to your father."

Carefully, Mercedes began to roll up the fragile parchment. "But how did my mother come to have this?"

"She must have taken it from Don Alejandro's safe," Longarm said. "You told me how sometimes her mind was clearer than others. She could have taken the land grant knowing that without it your father would lose his squabble with Tom McCabe."

"To punish him for bringing her to New Mexico, you mean?"

It was Longarm's turn to shrug. "Seems to me like it could've happened that way. Maybe one time while she was thinking straight, she planned to trade the document back to him in exchange for him taking her back to Spain. Then when she found out he'd had an affair with Nora Griffith, she decided to keep it away from him forever, so he could never get his hands on the land he wanted so bad."

"She knew what it would do to him to lose the land to McCabe," Mercedes said quietly. "He could have owned all the land in New Mexico except for that one piece, and if he thought it was rightfully his, he would never be at peace." She looked at Longarm. "You are right. You must be."

"Well, you have the land grant now," Emily said. "That pretty much settles things. When we get back, I'll legally transfer ownership of that property to your father. There won't be any more trouble." She glanced at Longarm. "You've really done your job now, Marshal."

Longarm smiled ruefully. He hadn't done this part of it. He'd been ready to ride away. Rosaria Canales was the one who deserved thanks for clearing up a decades-old mystery.

"This will actually make things simpler," Emily went on. "Now there's really no reason for Don Alejandro to know that he's my father. You have to give me your word, Marshal, that you won't tell him."

"All right," Longarm said. "You've got my word on it." If that was the way they wanted it, he supposed he could live with that. He took up the reins of the steeldust. "I reckon we'd better be riding."

On the heels of his statement he heard a distant crack, and something sang past his ear to strike the wall of Rosaria's home with an ugly thud.

Longarm's hand flashed to the butt of his Colt as he shouted, "Inside!" He didn't know where the shot had come from, but he was confident the thick walls of the hut would stop any more bullets.

Even as the three women turned toward the door, though, several more slugs kicked up dust in front of their feet. Mercedes cried out in fear. At the same time, Emily's chestnut mare threw its head up and gave a brief squeal of pain, a sound that was cut short as blood gushed from a wound in the animal's neck. At the smell of the gore, the other horses began dancing around frantically as the chestnut toppled over in death.

More bullets were whipping around them as Longarm grabbed Emily's arm with one hand and Mercedes's arm with the other. The gunfire had them cut off from Rosaria's house, but the old mission was close by, just a few yards down the street. "Into the church!" he shouted as he pushed the two young women toward the imposing building. He reached back, snagged the butt of his Winchester as the steeldust got ready to bolt, and jerked the rifle from its sheath. He ran after the women, glad to see that Rosaria was also following Emily and Mercedes.

The thunder of hoofbeats made him glance over his shoulder. He saw half a dozen men on horseback sweeping around from behind one of the other buildings and recognized Nash Lundy in the lead. Longarm threw the Winchester to his shoulder and snapped off a shot, but he knew even as he fired that he had missed. Then he turned and sprinted for the open door of the mission. The women were already scrambling through it and into the church.

Longarm was inside a second later, slamming the heavy door behind him and barring it. He went to one of the rifle ports built into the wall and peered out, then ducked instinctively as a lucky shot came through the opening and passed by him much too close for comfort. He waited tensely, hoping to spot a target of his own . . .

So that had been Lundy and some of Kingston's men, maybe even the rancher himself, following him and Mercedes from the north. Longarm had been afraid that was the case, although he had halfway hoped the dust cloud was being raised by some of Montoya's vaqueros. At least they wouldn't have killed Emily out of hand, the way Lundy would. And Lundy wouldn't stop until Longarm and Mercedes and Rosaria were dead, too. If he had enough men, he might even try to wipe out the entire village, just so no witnesses would be left behind.

Longarm grimaced. This was a bad spot, all right, and for the time being, all he and the women could do was wait.

He looked over his shoulder and saw that the three women had taken shelter behind the pews, as he had told them to do. Crouching, Longarm ran over to them and knelt beside Rosaria, who looked at him with wide, frightened eyes.

"Where's the padre?" Longarm asked. As far as he could tell, the mission was deserted.

"He is away, visiting the sick in the hills," Rosaria said. "He will not be back for several days."

Longarm nodded, glad to hear that the local priest wasn't going to be in any danger.

"Who are those men?" asked Rosaria. "Why do they want to kill us?"

"It's a long story," Longarm told her. "They're from the ranch next to Emily's. They ride for a man named Sam Kingston."

Rosaria nodded shakily. "I remember you mentioning him. How did they find you?"

"Followed us down here from New Mexico," Longarm said bitterly. "I didn't want to lead them to Emily, but I reckon that's just what I've done."

"You were trying to help, Marshal," Emily called over to him. "It's not your fault."

The hell it wasn't, Longarm thought. He had hoped he and Mercedes had given their pursuers the slip, but obviously that wasn't the case. Lundy was gunwise; he had probably split up his men and approached the village from several different directions so they would have all the possible escape routes covered. That way, the dust that had marked their location earlier had been dispersed, too. Longarm knew he and the women had been lucky to make it into the old church without being gunned down.

"Marshal! Hey, Marshal Long! I know you're in there!"

Longarm stiffened. There was no mistaking Sam Kingston's harsh, high-pitched voice. So the Diamond K owner had come along, too, on this killing mission, rather than entrusting it completely to Nash Lundy.

"Better come on out, Marshal, 'less'n you want some of the innocent folks in this here village to die!"

Rosaria's hand clutched at Longarm's sleeve. "This man, he would hurt the villagers?"

"Kingston'd do just about anything to get what he wants," Longarm replied grimly. "The men who are working in the fields, will they come back to the village when they hear the shooting?"

She nodded. "Yes, but most of them are not armed. They will have only pitchforks and hoes."

So they would be easy pickings for Kingston and his gunmen, thought Longarm. Unable to put up much of a fight to begin with, they would have to surrender out of fear of what might happen to their women and children if they didn't. In a matter of minutes, Kingston would have himself a whole village full of hostages, if he didn't already.

"What are we going to do, Custis?" Mercedes asked. "We cannot allow Kingston and his men to murder these people."

Before Longarm could answer, Kingston shouted again from outside. "Get out here, Long, and bring Miz McCabe with you!"

"I'll marry him," Emily suggested shakily. "I'll accept his proposal. And we can give him the land grant, too."

Mercedes looked like she might want to argue about that last part, thought Longarm, but it didn't really matter. He shook his head and said, "That wouldn't do any good. He's not interested in marrying you anymore, Emily. Not now that he's got a chance to see you dead."

"Long, take a look out one of them rifle ports! Nobody'll shoot at you! You got my word on that! I want you to see what I got here!"

Longarm started to get up. Rosaria clutched at him. "You believe that man?"

"Not for a second," Longarm replied grimly. "But I don't reckon I have much choice."

He stood up and moved toward the rifle port he had looked through before. Turning sideways to make himself a little smaller target, he edged up to it and carefully peered out.

Kingston and Lundy stood in the middle of the village's single street. The rancher was holding a rifle angled across his body. Next to him, Lundy had his left arm wrapped around the neck of a boy about ten years old. The barrel of the gun in Lundy's right hand was pressed to the boy's temple. Even from this distance, Longarm could see the expression of sheer terror on the boy's face.

"Long!" Kingston shouted again. "I'm gettin' impatient! You hear me in there?"

"I hear you," Longarm called back. "Tell that lapdog of yours to let the boy go!"

He saw Lundy stiffen, but Kingston motioned for the gunman to take it easy. Turning back toward the mission, Kingston said, "I don't want to have Nash kill this younker, Long, but I will if you and Miz McCabe don't get yourselves out here mighty quick-like!"

"So you can kill us?"

"Ain't nobody has to die," insisted Kingston. "We've just come to take Miz McCabe back home, that's all. Ever'body's worried 'bout her runnin' off like that."

"What proof do we have that you don't mean her any harm?" Longarm asked. He was just stalling now, but there was nothing else to do.

"Hell, I ain't never took back my marriage proposal. Montoya was the one what done that. I'd still like to marry up with the gal!"

From the pews, Emily hissed, "Marshal—"

"He doesn't mean it," Longarm said. "Don't think for a second that he does. If we step out there, they'll gun us both down without blinking. Then they'll finish off Mercedes and Rosaria and Lord knows who else."

From outside, Kingston shouted, "What's it gonna be, Long?"

"Hold on just a damned minute!" Longarm bellowed. He twisted his head to look at Emily. "Can you handle a rifle?"

She nodded. "I've been hunting with Tom. I can shoot all right, I guess."

"Rosaria, is there a way up into the bell tower?"

"Si," the older woman nodded. "There is a ladder in the nave. I can show you."

"Show Emily," Longarm told her. He stepped over to the pews and held the Winchester out to Emily. "Take this and climb up in the tower."

Her face was pale and drawn, but she nodded. "What do you want me to do?"

"If you can do it without them spotting you, once you get up there try to draw a bead on Lundy. Once I step outside, he'll likely forget about the boy and make a try for me. That's when you put a bullet in him."

"But . . . but if I miss, I might hit the boy. Or miss completely, and then Lundy will shoot you."

"I ain't going to be exactly defenseless myself," Longarm said dryly. "But I've got to draw Lundy's fire to give both you and the boy a chance."

Emily closed her eyes for a moment, then sighed and nodded as she opened them again. "All right. I'll try. But I wish Ross was here."

"Thayer? That dude lawyer?"

"He may be from back east, but he's the best rifle shot I've ever seen," Emily said.

Longarm frowned. "Is that so? Well, he ain't here, so it's up to you, Emily. I'll stall Kingston for a few minutes while you climb up in the tower."

"You can do it, Emily," Mercedes said. "I have faith in you."

Emily glanced at her. "You never even liked me before."

"That was before I knew we are sisters," Mercedes said with a shrug.

Longarm turned back toward the door of the church as Emily and Rosaria hurried toward the nave, where the ladder to the bell tower was located. He paused at the rifle port to shout, "Kingston! Tell your men to hold their fire! We're coming out!"

"Damn well about time!" Kingston replied. "Come ahead!" He shouted up and down the street, "Hold your fire, boys!"

Longarm heard the faint sounds of Emily climbing the ladder to the tower. He moved to the door and lifted the heavy bar that held it shut. He glanced back at Mercedes, who tried to smile encouragingly.

Rosaria stuck her head out of the nave, caught Longarm's eye, and nodded emphatically. Emily was in the bell tower. Longarm hesitated a moment longer, then reached for the door latch. He twisted it, pulled the door back, and stepped through the opening into the street.

Chapter 24

At that moment, everything seemed heightened to Longarm's senses. The heat of the sun, the smell of dust and spices that hung in the air, the stark contrast of light and shadow—all of it washed over him as time seemed to slow down. He saw distinctly the snarl of hate that twisted Nash Lundy's face and heard Sam Kingston shout, "No, the gal's not with him!"

Then it was too late, because everything was moving at its normal speed again and all it took was the blink of an eye for Lundy to jerk his gun away from the boy's head and point it at Longarm. Smoke and flame geysered from the barrel.

Longarm was already throwing himself to the side. As he moved, he heard the sharp crack of a rifle somewhere above his head. He saw the terrified boy jerk out of Lundy's grip and try to run, only to trip after a couple of frantic steps and fall sprawling in the street. The butt of Longarm's Colt bucked against his palm as he fired.

Lundy rocked back, struck first by Emily's shot and a split-second later by the slug from Longarm's gun. The gunman's bullet had whined past Longarm's shoulder to smack harmlessly into the door of the mission. As Lundy staggered, Longarm went to a knee and triggered a fast shot at Kingston, who was already returning the fire. Kingston's bullets kicked up dust in front of Longarm, blinding him momentarily.

Longarm flung himself into a rolling dive back toward the

door of the church. He heard Emily firing again from the bell tower, then the bell itself let out a deep, sonorous peal as something struck it. Longarm knew it must have been a bullet. Kingston's men, who were scattered around town behind cover, were opening up on the tower and the church.

From the corner of his eye, Longarm saw Kingston scramble behind an old cart that had been left on the street right where its axle had broken sometime in the past. Then Longarm was at the door and plunging through it into the church once again. He rolled over and planted a boot against the door, shoving it closed.

He was glad they had gotten Lundy, but he wished they could have downed Kingston, too. If the rancher and his segundo had both been dead, the rest of the gunmen might have given up. It was doubtful, but there would have at least been a slim chance. Now Kingston was bellowing curses outside. The loss of Lundy had to hurt, but Kingston wasn't just about to give up.

As Longarm hurriedly got to his feet and rebarred the door, Rosaria called from the nave in a panic-stricken voice. "Marshal! I think Señorita Emily is hurt!"

Longarm and Mercedes both rushed over to the older woman, who held out a hand smeared with crimson. "It drips from up above," she said, then pointed to smeared drops of blood on the floor.

The Winchester had fallen silent in the tower. Longarm tipped his head back and called up, "Emily!" There was no answer. Holstering his gun, he reached out to grasp one of the rungs of the ladder. He started climbing as quickly as he could.

If Emily was dead, he swore he would kill Sam Kingston himself, with his bare hands if necessary. All the tragic losses the young woman had suffered, followed by the shock of learning her true parentage, that was more than enough, Longarm thought. After all that, Emily didn't deserve to die here in this dusty little Mexican village.

He reached the massive brass bell and poked his head up so that he could look around the little platform inside the tower. It was built about four feet below the opening that ran around all four sides of the tower, under the tile roof. Emily was sitting with her back against the tower wall. Her eyes were closed, and the left side of her white blouse was red with blood.

Longarm pulled himself up on the platform and crawled over beside her. He put a hand to her throat and sent up a silent prayer of thanksgiving when he felt the pulse beating there raggedly but strongly. Carefully, he moved her left arm and saw that the wound was not in her side after all. A bullet had bored through the inside of her upper arm, a messy wound but not necessarily life-threatening. Still, she had lost enough blood so that she had fainted.

He leaned over the opening and called down, "She's alive!" Vaguely, he heard Rosaria's prayerful exclamation. Longarm yanked his bandanna from his pocket and wrapped it around the wound in Emily's arm, knotting it tightly in an effort to stop the bleeding.

She had dropped the Winchester beside her when she was hit. Longarm picked it up and thumbed fresh cartridges into it until its magazine was full again. Kingston and his men were still firing at the church, but they could waste all the powder and lead they wanted to, Longarm thought.

He took off his hat and tossed it aside, then carefully lifted his head over the top of the wall to scan the street. None of the gunmen were directing their shots up here anymore. When Emily was hit and the Winchester fell silent, they must have thought they had successfully disposed of that threat. Longarm spotted the barrel of a rifle poking out the door of a cantina down the street. He waited until the rifleman fired, then came up a little higher on his knees and drove a shot into the shadows just behind the muzzle of the gun. He heard a howl of pain and just before he ducked down behind the wall again, he saw a body come flopping out into the street.

Now the bullets started buzzing like a beehive around the bell tower again. Several of them ricocheted off the bell, setting up a tremendous racket. Longarm grimaced as the sound assaulted his ears. He wondered if it had been a ricochet that had hit Emily. That was likely, he thought, and the fact that the bullet was largely spent would have kept it from doing even more damage to her arm.

Kingston could win this battle by laying siege to the church, but Longarm had a feeling that wasn't what the rancher would do. A concerted rush would cost Kingston some more men, but when it was over the gunmen would be inside the church, killing everyone they found still alive. All Longarm could do was try to pick off as many of them as he could before the attack came. He waited until the firing died down, then risked another quick look over the wall.

What he saw didn't bode well. Kingston was gone from behind the abandoned cart, and Lundy's body was no longer lying in the street. Longarm wondered if Lundy was somehow still alive. He saw movement down the street, inside the shadows of a barn, and wondered if Kingston was gathering his men there for a charge. He thought about putting a few shots into the barn, but he realized he couldn't risk that. Until he was sure he was aiming at Kingston's men, he couldn't take the chance that he might be opening up on some of the villagers instead. Kingston's men could have herded them into the barn to keep them prisoner there.

Longarm started to sink back down below the level of the wall when something else caught his eye. There to the north, more dust rose. A good-sized group of riders had to be coming toward the village.

More of Kingston's men . . . or somebody else?

For the first time in a while, Longarm felt a spark of hope. He had thought all along that some of Montoya's men might try to find Mercedes, and if that was the case, then help might finally be on the way. The question was whether or not it would arrive in time, if it was coming at all.

He got his answer a moment later as a dozen or more men burst out of the barn and charged toward the church, firing and yelling as they came. From up and down the street, more rifle fire rattled as the rest of Kingston's men laid down covering fire for the attack. Longarm thrust the barrel of the Winchester over the wall and started shooting as fast as he could pull the trigger and work the rifle's lever. He tried to ignore the bullets buzzing around his own head as he poured lead into the wedge of killers pounding toward the mission.

A couple of them went down under Longarm's withering fire, but the rest of them came on. Powdersmoke wreathed the bell tower as he emptied the Winchester and then flung it aside. He pulled the Colt and leaned over to shout down to Mercedes and Rosaria, "Get up here now! I'll try to hold them off!"

The ladder was the only way into the bell tower. Longarm had quite a few cartridges left. He could make those bastards pay a heavy toll to get up here, he reflected. He reloaded the Colt's cylinder as Mercedes and Rosaria climbed the ladder and pulled themselves over onto the platform. The tower was small enough so that there was room for only one of them on each side, so they had the bell surrounded. Rosaria was breathing hard from the effort of the frantic climb, but she still leaned over to check on Emily, who was still unconscious.

A heavy pounding came from below. The gunmen were trying to batter down the door of the church. After a few minutes, a splintering crash told Longarm they had succeeded. Footsteps rang on the floor of the sanctuary. A harsh voice yelled, "Up there!"

Longarm waited until he heard men climbing the ladder, then poked the nose of the Colt over the edge and fired twice. A man yelled, and he heard crashing below as someone fell from the ladder and probably took more men with him as he plummeted to the floor.

"Get back!" he hissed to Mercedes and Rosaria.

They made themselves as small as possible as gunfire racketed from below. The bullets smashed into the bell, again causing a tremendous noise. If by some miracle he lived through this, Longarm thought, he might never want to hear a bell ringing again. Hell, he'd be lucky to be able to hear one, he told himself, because he was going to be deaf in about another minute.

The echoes from the horrible ringing were so loud and lingering that Longarm knew he couldn't hear the killers climbing the ladder anymore. He stumbled to his feet and glanced over the wall along the street. The band of riders that had been approaching the town a few minutes earlier had now reached the end of the street. The young man in the lead was wearing a broad-brimmed sombrero, but the wind created by his galloping horse had pushed the hat back off the rider's head so that it hung by its chin strap. Longarm recognized Chuy Valdez. Right behind him were more than a dozen of the Montoya vaqueros.

Valdez and the others had no way of knowing what they were riding into, but Kingston must have realized that he couldn't afford to let the vaqueros know that their *patron*'s daughter was holed up in the bell tower. Another volley ripped out from the hidden gunmen, and several of the vaqueros were knocked from their saddles. Valdez and his compadres, having already heard the shooting as they approached, had their guns out and ready. They returned the fire, sending a storm of lead into the hiding places of Kingston's hired killers.

Longarm cupped his hands around his mouth and yelled as loudly as he could, *"Valdez!"* The young vaquero wheeled his horse around, spotted Longarm in the bell tower, and spurred toward him. Several of the vaqueros followed him. Shots came from inside the church, but Valdez and the others came on relentlessly, triggering as they rode.

Mercedes screamed and Longarm spun back toward the open center of the tower in time to see one of the gunmen thrusting a pistol at him. Longarm's foot lashed out and caught the man on the wrist as the gun blasted. The shot went wild into the wall. Longarm slammed the barrel of his Colt down on top of the man's head. The killer's hat cushioned the blow, but it was still enough to knock him loose from the ladder. With a shriek, he fell, landing in a crumpled heap on the floor below.

He was the only one who had been on the ladder this time. The gunmen had learned something from their first attempt to reach the top of the tower. But they didn't have a chance for a third attempt, because Chuy Valdez and the other vaqueros rode their horses over the door that had been broken down earlier and sent the remaining killers spinning off their feet with well-placed shots. Longarm could see part of the action from where he was, and a moment later when the guns fell silent, he knew that Valdez and the other vaqueros had downed all of Kingston's men.

"Valdez!" Longarm called down. "Up here!"

Valdez leaped out of his saddle and swarmed up the ladder. As he reached the platform, he gasped breathlessly, "Señorita Mercedes—where is she?" Then his anxious gaze fell on Mercedes as she climbed shakily to her feet, and he swept her into his arms, hugging her fiercely and kissing her with a passion that brought a chuckle from Longarm. It looked like Mercedes had a secret admirer who wasn't so secret anymore. She was startled, but after a moment she began to return Valdez's kisses.

The young vaquero was a hothead, thought Longarm, but chances were he would settle down if he lived long enough—especially if he had something or someone to live for. Longarm had a hunch Valdez might do a good job of running Lariat one of these days.

Rosaria had slid over to Emily and pulled the young woman into her lap. Emily began to stir as consciousness came back to her. She blinked and looked up at Longarm. "Wh-where—"

"It's over," Longarm told her as he reloaded his gun again and slid it into its holster. "Some of Montoya's vaqueros rode up just in time and stomped the rest of Kingston's snakes."

Emily looked at the way Mercedes and Valdez were embracing and managed a faint smile. "Looks like I . . . missed a lot."

"Hush now, child," Rosaria told her. "You rest. You're going to be fine."

Longarm knelt beside them and quickly examined Emily's arm. "Yep, I'd say Rosaria's right. The bleeding's stopped. That arm'll be mighty sore for a while, but I expect it'll heal up just fine."

"Do you think we could . . . get down from here?" Emily asked weakly.

"I don't see why not. I'll go down the ladder first, but you come right after me so I can help you."

"And I will help from up here," Rosaria said.

Together, they got Emily down the ladder and helped her to lie down on one of the pews. Longarm made sure she couldn't see any of the sprawled corpses of Kingston's men from where she was. She had seen enough death for one day. They all had.

He left Rosaria watching over Emily and strode out of the church, noting the welter of bullet marks on the door as he did so. He had kept a war from breaking out in the valley up there in New Mexico Territory, but there had sure been one fought here today, he thought.

Esteban, Montoya's segundo, trotted up on horseback. "Marshal Long," he greeted Longarm. "You are all right?"

"Fine," Longarm said with a nod. "Ears are still ringing a

mite, but I reckon that'll go away. Did you get all of Kingston's men?"

"Is that who they were?" asked Esteban. "All we knew was that hombres were shooting at us." He shrugged. "So we shot back."

"You got here just in time. Kingston was after Emily McCabe, but Mercedes was holed up in there with us, too."

Esteban's eyes widened. "Señorita Mercedes, she is all right?"

Longarm nodded. "She's fine. She's up in that bell tower with young Valdez right now, finding out how he really feels about her."

Esteban rolled his eyes and laughed. "Chuy is a madman. He thinks that one day he will marry the *patron*'s daughter."

"I think he may be right," Longarm said. He trusted that Mercedes would have enough sense not to mention to Valdez what had happened between them on the way down here, or any of those other lovers she had supposedly had in Mexico City.

Longarm went on, "Have you seen Kingston?"

Esteban nodded. "He was guarding the people who live here while his men attacked the church. They turned on him when we rode in and began firing, and some of the men were able to get their hands on pitchforks and axes." For a moment, Esteban looked grim. "It was not pretty, what they did to him."

"Maybe not," said Longarm, remembering how casually Kingston had threatened to have Lundy blow that little boy's brains out, "but I reckon he had it coming."

Esteban looked around. "There was much damage done to this village. I think that Don Alejandro would like to see it put right."

"So would Mrs. McCabe, I expect. Maybe they could work together on it."

"A McCabe and a Montoya work together?" Esteban grinned. "Will such a thing ever happen?"

"You might be surprised," Longarm said with a grin of his own. He was turning back toward the church when the bloody figure of Nash Lundy came stumbling around the corner of the building. Lundy screamed a curse at Longarm, and the gun in his hand started to come up.

Longarm palmed out his Colt and fired a hair ahead of Lundy. The two explosions were so close together they sounded like one. Lundy's bullet drove into the ground at his feet, however, as Longarm's shot took him in the belly and doubled him over. Lundy's gun slipped out of his hand, and he pitched to the side.

Longarm kept his gun out as he strode over to Lundy's body, just in case. He hooked the toe of his boot under Lundy's shoulder and rolled him over. Lundy's eyes were open, but they were bleary and filled with pain. Life was rapidly slipping away from him.

Longarm knelt beside him, anxious to seize this opportunity to clear up one last detail. He said, "You should've bushwhacked me from long range, Lundy, the way you did with Tom McCabe."

An agonized laugh bubbled from Lundy's lips. "You stupid . . . bastard . . . I didn't shoot . . . McCabe."

Longarm nodded in satisfaction. "Didn't figure you did."

Lundy's eyes widened in understanding, then grew even wider as death claimed him. Longarm stood up.

Esteban said, "At least now it is truly over."

Longarm shook his head. "Nope. Not quite."

Chapter 25

Ross Thayer came onto the porch of the ranch house as Sheriff Orville Walcott brought the buckboard to a stop. Emily McCabe sat beside the sheriff on the seat, and Longarm rode alongside the wagon on the steeldust, which had come through the battle below the border unscathed.

"My God!" Thayer exclaimed as he rushed off the porch and reached up to take Emily's right hand. Her left arm was in a black silk sling. "Emily, are you all right? I was afraid I would never see you again."

"I'm fine, Ross," she told him. "I've got a bullet hole in my arm, but it's nothing."

"Nothing! Good Lord, you . . . you're hurt!"

Walcott said, "Settle down, counselor, and help the lady down from this buckboard. It ain't the smoothest ride in the world, you know, but it was all I could borrow in town."

"Why didn't you send word that you were back?" Thayer asked as he helped Emily climb down from the wagon. "I would have come for you in my buggy."

"I wanted to surprise you," Emily said.

Longarm swung down from the steeldust and tied its reins to a porch post. "Been making yourself right at home out here while Mrs. McCabe was gone, Thayer?"

The lawyer glanced at Longarm in irritation. "I assumed Emily would want someone to keep an eye on the place and make sure things were run properly in her absence."

"And you figure you could do a good job of running the ranch full-time, don't you?"

"What the devil do you mean by that?" snapped Thayer.

Emily put her hand on his arm. "Ross, we have news. The Montoya land grant has been found."

He looked at her, frowning in confusion. "What?"

"Don Alejandro really does own the land he and Tom argued over. I've seen the document with my own eyes. I'm going to legally transfer ownership of that area to him."

Thayer shook his head, clearly struggling to comprehend what Emily had just told him. "Montoya was in the right all along?"

"I'm afraid so." Emily managed to smile and shrug. "But even without that land, the Box MCC is a fine ranch, don't you think?"

"Of course. It's just a shame that . . . well, that there was all that trouble."

"Yes, but at least there will be peace now with Don Alejandro."

"So some good came of it all." Thayer smiled and put his arm around Emily's shoulders. "Why don't you come inside and rest? I'm sure you're tired after whatever happened to you while you were gone. I want to hear all about it—"

Emily pulled away from him. "You're being awfully forward, aren't you, Ross? After all, you're just my attorney."

Anger flared for a second in Thayer's eyes before he managed to conceal it and replace it with a look of hurt confusion. "Emily, why would you want to say such a thing? You know I'm more than that. I'm your friend. I've tried to help you ever since Tom died—"

Longarm drawled, "Yeah, it's mighty handy that you were around to take care of everything for Emily after McCabe was bushwhacked."

This time, Thayer didn't bother trying to conceal the anger that made his face flush. "I'm not sure what you're implying, Marshal, but I'm certain that I don't like it. You're a lawman, so you should be aware of the laws against slander."

"Ain't slander if it's true," Sheriff Walcott pointed out. "Got anything to say to that, counselor?"

Thayer looked around, his gaze going from Emily to Longarm to Walcott and finding none of them friendly at the moment. "What is this?" he asked. "We should be celebrating Emily's homecoming, yet the three of you are acting like it's some sort of inquisition."

Longarm said, "We were just wondering what you were doing out in the hills the day Tom McCabe died."

Thayer shook his head. "I wasn't in the hills. I was in town, in my office."

Emily said, "That's not what Warren told us."

"Warren? When did you talk to Warren?" Thayer glanced toward the house.

"He's not in there," Longarm said. "You shouldn't have ignored him so much, Thayer. Sheriff Walcott came out here last night and got him, brought him back into town so he could talk to us. He said he saw you up in the hills that day with a rifle. And Emily told me what a good shot you are."

"It's not true!" Thayer exclaimed. "You can't take the word of that . . . that dummy!"

"Warren's not a dummy," Emily said coldly. "He never has been. He's a sweet, simple man, yes, but he knows what he saw."

Walcott put in, "And I reckon there's a good chance a jury'll believe him, too."

Thayer began to back away from them. "This is insane!" he protested. "Warren couldn't have seen me that day! I made sure no one saw me—"

Longarm shook his head as Thayer stopped short. "Sometimes it's the fellas who figure they're the smartest who're the easiest to trip up."

Thayer's lips drew back from his teeth in a grimace. "You bastard!" he hissed. "You can't prove a damned thing. And I don't care what you say, no jury is going to take Warren McCabe's word over mine."

"I don't care about a jury," Emily said. "*I* know the truth now, Ross. I know that you killed my husband. You thought that in my grief I'd turn to you, and eventually you would marry me and take over the ranch. You almost succeeded. I never even suspected you, even though I knew what a good shot you are." Her voice began to tremble with anger and bitterness. "You were so *good* to me, I thought. I believed you just wanted to help me."

"I did!" Thayer practically shouted. "That was all I ever wanted, Emily!"

She took a step toward him, shaking now. "Get off my ranch," she said in a low, dangerous voice. "I'm going to give the men orders that if you ever set foot on McCabe land again, they're to shoot you like they would a rabid coyote. The same holds true for Lariat. Don Alejandro gave me his word."

Thayer began shaking his head. He was pale, and his once handsome face had turned haggard. "You can't do that," he croaked.

"I reckon she can," Sheriff Walcott said. "Havin' a fella shot for trespassin' is a mite severe, I reckon, but I don't figure any court in these parts would ever indict Miss Emily. You might as well light a shuck, Thayer. Once word gets around about what you done—and it will—you'll be washed up for good in this valley. Probably in the whole durned territory."

Thayer swung his stunned, furious gaze toward Longarm. "This is your doing, you son of a bitch," he accused. "You're the one who made up that filthy pack of lies!"

Longarm shrugged. "Once I was convinced none of Montoya's men had anything to do with Tom McCabe's death, and then I got a dying statement from Nash Lundy that he didn't do it, that just left one good suspect. What Warren told us clenched it for us."

"I tell you he didn't see me," grated Thayer.

"You'll never know, will you, old son?" Longarm asked mildly.

Thayer broke then, launching a punch at Longarm's head. Longarm swayed aside and easily avoided the blow. He brought his right fist around and smashed it into Thayer's face. The lawyer went flying backward to crash against the front porch. He bounced off and fell to his hands and knees.

Longarm turned toward Emily, grinning as he massaged the knuckles of his right hand with his left. "That felt even better than I figured it would—"

A long-barreled gun appeared suddenly in Walcott's hand and boomed loudly. Emily cried out and put a hand to her mouth. Longarm turned around and saw Thayer hanging against the porch where the sheriff's bullet had driven him, blood on his shirt front and a small pistol dangling from his fingers. The gun slipped from his hand and thudded to the ground, and a second later the lawyer pitched forward on his face to lie motionless.

Walcott glowered at Longarm. "If I thought you turned your back on him a-purpose so's he draw on you and make me kill him, I'd be a mite peeved with you, Marshal."

"Much obliged to you for saving my life, Sheriff," Longarm said.

Walcott snorted and holstered his pistol.

Longarm took Emily's arm and turned her toward the house, away from the sprawled body. Thayer had been right about one thing—Emily needed some rest. She was going to be mighty busy for a while making friends with Don Alejandro Montoya instead of fussing with him.

And maybe someday, she would be ready to tell him the truth. Longarm sort of hoped so. But either way, he would be long gone from this valley by then.

He stretched like a big cat. Clean, cool sheets felt mighty nice.

So did what was going on down around his groin.

Soft, warm lips wrapped themselves around the head of his manhood, and a tongue darted tantalizingly around the slit. Estellita Rafferty's mouth opened even wider as she swallowed more of his shaft.

Longarm kept his eyes closed and sighed in contentment. He had stayed over in Palmerton one more night, since it had been too late to start back to Santa Fe, and he was glad he did. Lita had climbed through the window of his hotel room, and before they had gotten down to what she had come there for, she had told him that her father no longer hated him, now that he had saved Mercedes Montoya's life and brought about peace between the Box MCC and Lariat.

"And I could never be angry with you, Custis," she had told him as she closed her hand around the thick pole of male flesh jutting up in readiness. "Not as long as you have this."

"So you just love me for my body, eh?" Longarm asked with a laugh.

"Shut up and put that big thing inside me."

Now, after a night of lovemaking, Longarm was surprised to find that he could still get so hard, so fast. Lita brought out the best in him, he supposed. He opened his eyes and raised up enough to see her coppery curls bobbing up and down above his hips as she continued the French lesson.

Longarm took a deep breath and held it as he felt his climax seize him. His organ throbbed as it launched spurt after spurt of his hot seed into Lita's eager mouth. When he fell back onto the bed, she milked the last drop from him and lapped it up. She turned her head and looked at him with a smile as she asked, "Would you like to come down to the cantina for breakfast?"

"Plenty of hot peppers in the scrambled eggs," Longarm gasped. He was going to need their restorative powers.

Watch for

LONGARM AND THE MOUNTAIN BANDIT

267th novel in the exciting LONGARM series
from Jove

Coming in February!